Hannah-Mariah, Bear-Angel To the Rescue

by

Maureen Rooseboom

AmErica House
Baltimore

First printing

ISBN 1-58851-762-4
PUBLISHED BY AMERICA HOUSE BOOK PUBLISHERS
www.publishamerica.com
Baltimore

Printed in the United States of America

This book is dedicated to my mother, who convinced me to dare to follow my dreams, and to my father, who instilled in me a love of books.

Chapter 1

"Why did we have to be born on New Year's Eve?" Nell Kylahy asked her twin brother, Luke, as they watched Home Alone on their big screen television.

"I don't know, Nell. But, I like the idea that we were the very last day of the year—not the first. Would you want to be in the paper as the 'First Babies of the New Year'?"

"No. I guess that'd be worse. I just wish we were born on an ordinary day- like, you know, February 5th or November 28th or October 7th. Do you know what I mean, Luke?"

"Yeah!" Luke said as he clicked off the TV and stretched back further on the dark teal-blue reclining chair. "I sure do! But, we can't do much to change the fact we were born on New Year's Eve."

"I know. Every year, Ma and Dad make such a big deal over it. I think they go overboard a bit much because they don't want us to feel left out that the evening's a biggie for everybody—the 'Ring in the New Year' stuff and all that."

"Hey, Nell, I wish we could do something really different on our birthday instead of the same old thing—a cake after supper, then the gift-giving and—"

"—then, Ma and Dad going to the New Year's Eve Party, don't forget."

"Oh, yeah! And, this birthday is our most important one, Nanny says, because we're ten. We've lived a whole decade! Wow, like I care!"

"I know, Luke. I feel the same way. I suppose we should get excited because the family does." She leaned over and grabbed the bag of her favorite Lay's Potato Chips—Classic, and started to munch them, as she waited for Luke's reply.

"Yeah . . . but you know, having been around ten years, I think we're pretty smart. We don't need a big deal bein' made of our 'End of Year' Birthday."

"I hear you. The thing that really bothers me is our friends' teasing us about when we were born."

"Do the girls rat on you like the guys do on me?"

"Yeah. I guess you could say they do. They're more—what's our big deal Vocab word, we had a few weeks ago with Mrs. McCaragh, that means 'hint, don't come outright with'?"

" 'Subtle', the adjective, or 'subtly', the adverb. I think that's a great word—or, they both are for that matter, Nell!"

"Yeah. I like them, too. I love Vocab and Reading! Mrs. McCaragh makes these subjects fun! She's a great teacher!"

"She sure is! Remember that story we read last week about going into the future. I wish we could go back into the past."

"Get real! Why would you wanna do that, Luke?"

"I'd like to know what it was like when we were born, or even go further back if we could, just for awhile."

"How 'bout we step into the future—what with our entering the Millennium?"

"Why? I don't want to see into the future. That'd scare me. I'm content to be living in the present, although a side trip into the past now and then might help us to understand things."

"You know, maybe you're right," Nell answered, then hesitated a moment before switching the subject.

"Hey, Luke, I'm a little worried about Dad and Ma goin' out to celebrate tonight. I sure hope Ma drives home. Even though it's only about a forty minute ride, I'm still concerned."

"Don't worry. They'll be okay. Ma will drive if he drinks too much. We'll have Auntie Leonore and Uncle Tom here with us. They're cool!"

"Yeah, that they are!" Nell said with enthusiasm, trying to get her mind on her aunt and uncle rather than let it stay on her dad.

It didn't work, however, because Luke's next remark brought them back onto the issue that concerned them both. "They've helped us through some tough times, haven't they, Nell?"

"I'll say! They know and we know, but I don't think Ma has a clue just how bad Dad's drinking problem is. After all we've read and learned and from what Auntie and Uncle say, Dad is an alcoholic."

"Dad doesn't think so, though. Some of my friends have dads or moms or other relatives who really get so drunk they fall down flights of stairs, throw things around or push people and hit them. They lose their jobs and sometimes the alcoholic loses his family because they can't take his drinking anymore."

"You know, Luke, I think he really thinks he's a 'social drinker,' that he can have a few drinks at a party and that's that. He's fine when he gets home and sleeps it off."

"I think we should tell him what we think. But, maybe, we should clue Ma in first. Ask her to join us and go along with what we're saying and let him know it bothers her, too."

"Why? What good would it do? Every time we've asked them not to go drinking Dad always says, 'I have to. I have my image to uphold. What would my boss think if I didn't?' "

"That's true—but, sooner or later our bugging him by telling him what it's doing to him and to us has gotta sink through."

"You know, Nell, at school we get all these lectures from our Counselor on 'self-esteem' and how 'peer pressure can lower it'. Ms. Pelicano says it's at our age that this happens the most. I say NO WAY! Look at grown-ups. Look at Dad! Right?"

"I know. But, how can we reach him? Is there some way we can make him see how he's hurtin' his family, how we worry about him getting worse, and maybe losin' his job and—"

"Why don't we go out and get some fresh air and maybe we can think of something?" he cut in, with an anxious look on his face. He feared his mother just happening by.

"Okay. Give me a couple minutes to get changed over."

Nell ran up the beautiful oak stairs, which were covered in a blue heather Berber rug. The very pale blue-gray walls matched the runner both up the staircase and in the hall above, where the rug was also carried.

She changed from her casual sweats into something warmer; a pair of jeans and her favorite blue nylon insulated jacket Nanny Yakonis had embroidered her name on.

Meanwhile, downstairs, Luke grabbed his new red winter parka; proud of the nice embroidered touch on his. He liked his name written on it. He felt like a member of a pro-ball team.

He slipped on heavy socks and his hiking boots. He knew Nell would want to go walking to their favorite place, the woods behind their house. These were their woods, a part of their property. They loved to explore every nook and cranny of this forest behind their beautiful pale gray colonial home with blue shutters, as much as they enjoyed playing on their huge front lawn, with its pretty flower gardens, rocks and trees.

Far, far back, they had a clubhouse of sorts set up. It was their private place.

They had to jump on the huge flatish rocks to cross the meandering stream to get there. They could go further along and eventually hop over it, but it was more fun to do the rock jumping, more of a challenge, an adventure. And, they both loved adventure.

Chapter 2

As the children started out down their backyard, their mother spotted them and yelled, "Where do you guys think you're going?"

"We're just taking a little walk, Ma," Nell called up to her. We won't be gone long. We promise. And, we won't fall into the stream. Okay?"

"Okay, but you should've said something to me before heading out. What if I didn't see you leavin' right now? You know Dad and I would've been worried. Don't be out there too long, you hear me? Remember tonight."

The twins responded in unison, "We remember."

And so their trek into the woods was marred by the fact that someone else knew where they were going. It was always more of an adventure if they could sneak away without anyone knowing. Then, they felt like they were really on their own—and, far, far away—not just imagining magical places in their own backyard.

As they walked along toward the stream, Luke seemed a bit down and Nell quickly picked up on it.

"Luke, what's the matter? You seemed all excited about getting out here a few minutes ago, and now it's like . . . you could care less that we're going out to our special spot. How come?"

"I don't know. I think Ma's reminding us of tonight kind of put a damper on my excitement."

"Come on. That's no way to be. We can still have a good time! Forget tonight! Let's pretend we're somewhere else—in a far distant land—like we always do. Where would you like to be?"

"Nell, you know, sometimes it's not that easy to jump from happy to sad and back again," he responded, as he hopped over some fallen tree branches.

"Well, you just jumped from happy to sad pretty fast. Why not go back to happy again just as quickly?"

"I don't know. For me, I guess it's always easier to change the other way around. Once I'm down, it's hard to get out of it."

"I know. You've always been like this. I understand, Luke."

"You know, Nellie, parents sometimes act as if they're the only ones who have down times and days. Do you think they believe we can, too?"

"I'm sure they're aware of it. They probably don't want us to know that they are. They probably don't know how to deal with it—a child being 'blue'." She skirted around a large gray rock and bent to avoid a blue spruce's wide branch, hanging over their path, as she talked.

"That could be it! I know they both love us, Nell! They tell us they do and show us how much all the time."

"Yeah, that's true! They do! And, we love them a whole lot, too! I just wish we could find a cure for Dad's sickness, his alcoholism!"

"I know. But, you know, maybe someday someone will. It's something that can be 'arrested'. How's that for a good word? They say it's hereditary. I hope you and I don't become alcoholics."

She caught up with him, grabbed his upper arm and got in his face, as she said, "Look, Luke. We'll never touch the stuff because we hate it. We see what its doing to Dad, don't we?"

"Yeah, you got that right. I do hate the booze! Just the smell on his breath turns my stomach. I wouldn't tell Dad and I try not to show him what effect it has on me because I don't want to hurt his feelings. Remember, he thinks he's 'in' because he can drink with the best of them. He can 'hold his liquor'. Well, sometimes I see him, and I'm not so sure."

"That was a pretty good speech, if ever I heard one! I agree with you. He can't."

"Well, it wasn't meant to be a speech, Nell. I admit I can 'expound'—another good word?—on this subject once I get going."

"I know. I feel the same way. We'll think of a way of helping him once we get to our Magic House."

"I sure hope so! It'd be wonderful if he didn't drink! It'd be a dream come true!"

"I'll second that!" she said, as they neared the rippling stream that curved through the thickly clustered pine trees.

They continued to trudge along, through the dappled sun-lit woods in silence now, alone with their thoughts. They had let out their feelings non-stop from their backyard to the brook.

The bluebirds and chickadees that only moments before were chirping crazily, now seemed to quiet down, as they sensed Luke and Nell's approach.

Usually, they came into their private hideaway stealthily, pretending they were large cats or other animals. Now, because they were heavy-hearted, their feet reflected that heaviness.

* * *

Nell peeked in the door they had built out of old logs and brushed aside the small branches that were bent and broken from their going in and out.

It was a very small opening. They didn't need a large one, as they were able to fit through just fine. They tried to cover it over with branches when they left so that no animals would get in.

Luke sat on his flat log seat and looked up at Nell. She glanced at the old chalkboard they had taken from their Playroom because they had a new bigger one there now.

Neither of them had taken any notice of the small table they had pieced together out of logs, with a flat stone for a tabletop.

Nell started to look for the little box of colored chalk they left here, wondering if the chalk would still write because of the cold and wet snow that had melted on the ground.

Luke went to put his head down in his hands and prop his elbows on the table when he noticed the mirror, a small oval-shaped silver mirror, with little silver stars all around its perimeter. The stars were gleaming like real stars in the night sky. It was semi-dark in the hut, so they showed up really well.

After Nell finally found a few pieces of the chalk in a corner near their Hidden Treasures Box, she looked around and started to tell Luke, "Okay, let's have a Brainstorm Session ov—" She never finished what she was going to say because when she looked around she saw Luke sitting at the table, looking totally dumbstruck. He was staring at something shiny in front of him, with his eyes bugging out of his head and his mouth wide open.

She leaned over his shoulder to see more clearly and what she saw totally took her breath away. Her mouth went dry. She couldn't speak, even though she tried.

"L-Luke, L-L-Luke," she barely scratched out. "Wha— What's th-that?" she stuttered.

"A mirror, Nell. You know what it is. You have one of these on your bureau."

"Oh, no, I don't! Nothing like that! Do you see what it's doing?"

"No, I just shut my eyes and pretend that this isn't real. Of course, I see what it's doing. This is cool, really cool!" he whispered, without moving a muscle.

"Luke—the stars—they're like real—I mean REALLY REAL! Look at the way they're taking turns shining. This is spooky!" Nell said, softening the tone of her voice to match Luke's. She was leaning on his shoulders for support, as she felt a little weak.

"Hey, why don't we take this outside and see if it'll reflect in the water?" Luke asked.

"Okay," Nell answered, as she looked at the mirror anxiously. "You wanna carry it?"

"Sure. Let's go!" Luke picked up the small mirror with the even smaller silvery stars. It felt warm in his hand. He didn't tell Nell because he didn't want to make her more nervous than she already was.

The children went over to the stream. It was a lot lighter outside than in their Magic House. They held the mirror over the water and saw that it didn't do much reflecting. So, they decided to lay it on the big flat boulder beside them. Maybe it needed a rest.

As they sat here with their eyes on the starry mirror, they started to gab.

"You know, Luke, I wish we could be animals. I'd love to be a bear!"

"Me, too! How come?"

"Well, bears don't have birthdays to worry about. Oh, they do have them. They were born sometime, but they don't celebrate them, ya know?"

"And, they don't do alcohol, so they wouldn't worry about their parents becomin' addicted," Luke chimed in. "You know, Nell, I'd love to be a bear because then we could survive out here in the forest. We wouldn't worry about—here's another one of Mrs. McCaragh's Vocab words—'predators'. We could take care of ourselves, unlike cats in the woods, that is, 'domestic'—another one of our words—cats. The bigger cats do just fine."

As they talked, a dark gray cloud came and hovered right over them. All of a sudden, they were in the middle of a snow squall. They laughed because they could hardly see one another and they were sitting pretty close together on the rock.   N e l l stuck her tongue out to catch the big flakes and Luke held his hands out to see how many landed in a minute.

"Nell, let's get in our hut. This stuff's really comin' down," he yelled, as he started to run back. Nell ran behind him and passed him through the doorway.

Chapter 3

After they wiped the flakes off their hair and jackets, they sat and smiled.

"Remember why we came out here, Luke?"

"Oh, yeah. I did lose track of our purpose. Carry on, then. You can do the notes for this Brainstorming Session."

"Okay. How should we go about this? Just jot down thoughts, words, ideas, like we usually do? Or, do you wanna try somethin' different?"

"How about we make two lists? We label the one on the left—'Problems' and the one on the right—'Solutions'?"

"That sounds good, Luke. Okay—what's our first problem goin' to be?"

"Well, how about we head it first?"

"Sure. What should our heading be?"

" 'New Year's Resolutions on Helping Dad'," he said seriously, and with a little more optimism than usual.

"Okay! Great, Luke!"

The children sat huddled over their makeshift table with the little blackboard in hand. They could hear the wind howling outside of their hut. The cold draft and some of the squall's snowflakes were coming through the cracks in the door and in between the boards they'd pieced together.

"Don't you just hate it when Dad says he has to go out and dreams up an outlandish chore he has to do?" Luke asked, with a grown-up look of knowing on his face.

"Yeah. You wanna put that down for Number 1? Is it a problem we can work on?"

"Okay. Put it down. Since I thought of a problem, you should think of a solution for it, Nell."

"Well, I know we all get scared. Ma, too. That look comes into her eyes that says, 'No way! You're not foolin' us!'. The poor little darling says, 'Okay, let's go! I can get such and such' and we can get something she could care less about. She just dreams it up so he won't take the truck alone."

"That's funny in a way, because Dad doesn't know what to do. How can he tell her, 'I don't want you with me'?"

"We can hide the keys so he can't reach for them and head for it before Ma even knows he's gone."

"Yeah, that's good! Put it as our Solution Number 1. Dad just doesn't seem to understand our fear of him and the truck together. What a deadly combo! If he doesn't kill himself, he could kill someone else. We'd certainly lose the house, Ma said, if he hurt other people, not to mention the horrible way he'd feel when he sobered up. We would, too! It's not somethin' any of us could live with, huh?"

"You're right, Luke. I wouldn't want anything to happen to Dad or anyone else! Hey, how about for another problem—when Dad brings home the liquor and hides it?"

"You mean in the ceiling rafters in the cellar? Well, all we can do about that is keep ditching it when we discover it on our little hunts. I say we should throw it down the sink in front of him!"

"But, he'd get mad, Luke. He'd start his hollering and swearing, and you know how nervous that makes Ma?"

"Yes, but if he could see how determined we are, that just might do the trick."

"I guess we could give it a shot. I don't believe he keeps hiding the stuff in the same old place! Heck, we can see the bulge in his coat pocket where he's carrying it. Sometimes, he's left it there because he hasn't had a chance to hide it yet. I've taken it from his jacket and ditched it."

"Me, too, Nell. He gets so nervous. You'd think we were taking a million dollars and throwing it away."

"Yeah! He does get shaky, but that's the booze! It's in him and it makes him crazy. Addiction is a powerful thing. It takes hold of you, you know what I mean?"

"I hear ya, Nell. Hey, you ready for Problem Number 3?"

"Let's hear it, Luke."

"How 'bout when he shouts and swears at all of us when he returns from drinking on a Friday night or at a party?"

"We could take Ma and the keys to the car and the truck and go out—just leave him," Nell answered confidently, as if she had the perfect solution for this one.

"Okay. If we do that, who's mindin' the house? Suppose he smokes and drinks and falls asleep. It's happened before. Remember the couch in the den? You smelled the smoke and alerted Ma and me and we high-tailed it downstairs so fast. We got Dad off of it and brought pots of water and poured them all over it. The alarms were a waste. Dad pulled those out because he didn't like the screeching sound. We should have Ma get some fire extinguishers, though."

"Yeah, we should! Do you remember what we did with that couch, Luke?"

"We just turned the cushion upside down. There's another one there that matches it from long ago."

"Well, when you live with an alcoholic, there's a lot of things that don't get done, that are neglected. Look at me, Luke, my teeth. They're crooked because I sucked my thumb, even when my new teeth started to come in in Second Grade. Ma tried everything to get me to stop it. She even put on that hot peppery stuff the doctor recommended, but nothing helped. Why? Because I'm nervous. And, poor Ma doesn't realize how crooked they are. She has bigger problems to worry about."

As she was talking, she started to tear up. She had been doing a good job holding in her pain and the tears burst forth when she added, "And, poor Dad. Sometimes, he'll look at me and say, 'Your poor little teeth, Darly. We gotta do something about them.' "

Luke leaned over and gently hugged her. He had tears building up in his eyes, too. He wanted to make her laugh and forget her crooked teeth.

"Hey, Nellie! Look at me! Look at my poor fingertips. I nibble 'em when I'm nervous. That's my bad habit. I can put Band-Aids on them when they bleed. But, I understand how you feel. It's tough! I know you're embarrassed. I see you smile and try not to show them with people. But, you can't be like that! Someday, once we get Dad to be okay, we'll get them to get you to the orthodontist. All right, little Sis? What do ya think?"

Nell looked over at him and tried to smile. "I'm so lucky I've got you! Can you see either of us bein' an only child, Luke? Thanks! You're right. Let's straighten out his problem, then we can work on ours. And, you're right again—those are nasty-lookin' fingertips. Yuck!" she ended, giggling at his hands, as he tried to fold his fingers into his palms so she'd stop kidding him about them.

"All right, where were we? We never found a solution for Number 3. Why can't we let that one go and try to think of another one for now? We can always come back and finish it later. Okay?"

"Fine!" Nell said as she put her mind on trying to think of a fourth problem. "I got it! How 'bout if Dad ever says he needs help?"

"That's a good one. What'll we do?"

"Get him to an AA Meeting! Fast! Before he changes his mind!"

"You know, Nell, I hear those meetings are pretty good. Zack and Shauna were saying their parents have taken them to Anniversary Meetings, and there was always a ton of food. They said all the people there were so nice and friendly. They were treated like long-lost relatives. And, I guess, from what they said, when the speakers get up and talk, it's really sad."

"Yeah. I know. Shauna told me the speakers say they're alcoholics and then they tell all about their lives and what their drinking has done to them and their families. Some of them start cryin' and the people who are listenin' cry, too. They've all been through similar problems. That's why they're so close."

"But, it does the alcoholics good to let it out—to strangers. You know, some people can open up to strangers in a way they never can to their own families, Nell."

"I know, Luke. But, the people at these meetings soon become like a family. You know, sometimes, your own relatives just don't understand what you're goin' through. Whereas, someone who's gone through the same thing does. They can empathize."

"That's true. Even for us kids. I tell you everything, but it's probably because we've been through so much together. I know a lot of brothers and sisters who are closer to friends. They don't tell anyone in their families their deepest darkest secrets. At least, we have each other!"

"Yeah, I'm grateful. You're a pretty cool brother! I guess I'll keep you!" she laughed, as she thought about the very close bond they did have because of their father's drinking problem. They may not have been so close, if there weren't a problem they shared.

"You know, Nell. I just wish Dad could tell his boss off, and his so-called 'friends', who hit him with, 'Hey, Mike, come on! Ya gotta have a drink! Just one!' I'm sure they know that for alcoholics the 'just one' is all it takes. They can't stop at that."

"Luke, I think grown-ups are worse than kids, at times. They get him drinking because they are, and you know the old saying, 'Misery loves company'. If they're feelin' lousy, they want someone else to feel lousy, too. You know there are kids like that—some of our classmates? Luckily, we're wise enough to avoid them. There are enough nice kids around so that we can pick our friends. I'd rather have one or two close ones than try to get everyone to be my friend. That's not being realistic!"

"I hear ya and I agree! Hey, how about Problem Number 5? What do you—"

Nell interrupted what he was going to say as a thought hit her.

"Oh, dear, Luke! It just dawned on me. We completely forgot about that beautiful mystical mirror in our rush to take shelter from the snow squall!"

Chapter 4

They hurried for the tiny opening they called their door and rushed out into the snow-covered brambles and bushes that were under their feet.

"Oh, no! It'll be all covered with snow. I don't think it likes the wet!" Luke said, as he stumbled his way down to the stream.

"You talk as if it's a person, it's alive!" Nell added, a little out of breath from rushing up and out so quickly.

"That mirror seems it to me! I don't know why, but there's something eerie about it. Although, I still say it's cool!"

They hurried over to where they remembered leaving the mirror on the stone.

At first, they couldn't see it because enough snow had fallen in the short amount of time the squall lasted to completely cover something so small.

All of a sudden, they knew where it was because different rays of colored light, like a rainbow—were shining through the snow, leading them right to it.

When Nell went to grab the little mirror, something really strange happened. A star shot off of it and headed straight up, but not too high. Then, a second star did the exact same thing. The children didn't know what to make of it!

The two stars hovered above them, as the rest of the mirror dimmed. They looked like they were trying to get the children to follow them—the way a dog will keep coming back to his owner and start running a bit in a certain direction and then keep repeating this action, until the owner follows him.

Finally, Luke, looking fascinated, said, "Well, I think we should follow the blinking stars. Don't you, Nell?"

"Yeah, I guess so. Let's go!"

So, they followed the stars as they shot their light through the forest. The light they gave off was a glowing rainbow haze of brightness with streaks attached. They'd seem to be way ahead of the twins one minute and then be right in front of them the next.

They found themselves going up a little hill way out in the woods, as they continued to try to catch up with the silvery shining stars. Just when they thought their journey would be through, the stars would jut up, up and away once more.

"It seems like we've been walking forever," Nell said, as she started to tire out.

While she was completing her comment, the stars started to float ahead of them to the top of this hill. They trudged up the final few feet to a vast clearing.

As they stood here, they saw the most beautiful little house they could imagine, set off on the distant side of this wide-open area.

It was all fieldstone. It had a natural wooden frame over the silvery portal, with two stone steps in front.

The children noticed the side window as they approached, and saw that there were pink shutters on each side of the window. The shutters were the color of strawberry ice cream. And, there were sky-blue curtains hanging on this tiny window in this very small house.

What was really fascinating were the roses—all shades of pink, growing up wild-looking vines under the window. It couldn't be, they both thought. Roses didn't grow in January in Atkinson, New Hampshire.

Shooting down from the wooden roof were vines, which seemed to be hanging from the tiny fieldstone chimney. And, way up on the chimney, a little blue-bird was sitting, singing a cheery song of welcome.

Luke and Nell were taken aback. They stopped dead in their tracks. They were afraid to go any further.

Nell started to proceed up the narrow dirt path, which didn't have an ounce of snow on it, even though they just had the snow squall.

Luke reached out and grabbed her arm to stop her and said anxiously, "No, Nellie! I don't like the looks of this! Let's turn around and get outta here!"

"What're you talkin' about, Luke? This is beautiful! It's fantastic! Look, roses and—"

"Nell, are you nuts?" he interrupted, with an unbelieving look on his face. "This can't be real! That's just it! It's too beautiful, and roses aren't supposed to be growing now! It's winter! Come on!"

"Luke, Luke, Luke, where's your sense of adventure?"

"It just got up and left me!"

"Come on! Something drew us here and I think we should take a peek inside this little house. We can sneak up around the side and look in that little window. I think there's an opening in those curtains. They're not drawn tightly."

"You are certifiable! Nuts! Let's go now, Nell, while the getting's good. I'm gettin' a funny feeling. This just isn't real!"

"So what! Is that so bad, Luke? What kind of feeling are you getting? Is it a bad one? Are you getting bad vibes? You have been down all afternoon."

"No," he answered, after contemplating the questions she hit him with. "I honestly can say what I'm sensing isn't a bad feeling. It's actually quite peaceful. That's why I don't trust it."

"What do you mean you 'don't trust it'?" she asked with a baffled look.

"Well, Nell, you know the old saying, 'If it seems too good to be true, it probably is'."

"Yeah, but I think if it feels good and you feel at peace, which I do, too, we should take a look. We'll be cautious, Luke. I know Ma and Dad drilled a lot of that 'Be Careful' stuff into us. I'm not crazy! I'm just curious."

"Typical woman!"

"Now, now, Luke, that's not fair! That's being sexist! Guys are just as nosey. The only difference is you just don't want to let us girls know. You try to disguise your inquisitive natures."

"I know. You're right. I was just trying to pick on you because you're acting braver than I am, now. And, that ticks me off because according to the old sexist theory we learned about this year, we men were always supposed to be the 'Brave Ones'. Hah!"

"Luke, I'm no braver than you are. My curiosity or nosiness just happens to be stronger at the moment. It does sometimes get the better of me. We both have equal amounts of courage and curiosity. They just come out at different times and in different circumstances. We may be twins and think a lot alike about some things, but our feelings and reactions to new things aren't always the same."

"That's true. You do make sense, Nell. Okay, let's go for it! But, please, let's take it slowly."

"Okay. What do you suggest? We just go up to that beautiful silver door and tap on that knocker or we sneak around to the side?"

"I say, we 'Take the bull by the horns', as the expression goes, and head for the door."

"Wow, we are getting brave, dear brother of mine!" Nell said, with a proud expression on her face and a big smile.

"Well, the sooner we look into this, the sooner we'll know."

Nell stared at him, with a questioning look. "That's certainly a logical statement," she said with a teasing smile, hoping to alleviate Luke's nervousness.

She knew he was drilled in Dad's sexist mentality, where the guy must always protect the girl. Some things didn't change through the generations in families. Dad was certainly brave, she thought, but so was Ma.

Just then, Luke decided to step up the path first—to show her he was conquering his initial fear of this interesting house. "Aren't you coming?" he asked, with a smile on his lips that was matched by one in his twinkling baby-blue eyes.

She laughed and started to follow because underneath her show of bravado lurked a small amount of skepticism about whether or not they should approach. Yes, she had her fears, too. But, she tended to be more headstrong, sometimes letting her feelings, whatever they might be, get in the way of thinking things through clearly.

When they made it to the front door, they noticed that it was a mirror and on this mirror-covered door were words written in a sky-blue scroll that matched the pretty curtains on the two side windows. 'Angels are forever friends,' the mirror-covered door read.

"Okay, Nell. I think it's time to bug out. This is too much! We're both crazy! Do you see what I see?" he muttered under his breath, afraid to turn and look at her.

"Yes, I do. That's a cute saying. So, what? Lots of people believe in angels and have dolls and pictures and this kind of stuff in their homes."

"Yeah, but, Nell, on your front door? Come on! Let's bolt! I sense something strange."

"Well . . . I have to admit this is different, but-"

Just as Nell was about to defend the strange-looking door, it opened.

Chapter 5

The twins were so shook they just stood there with their eyes bugged out and their mouths wide open. They immediately drew closer together, hugging one another.

They stared at the creaking door that was lined with old pine boards and heard a pleasant motherly voice, coming from within the little cottage. "Hello, please come inside," were the words they picked up on, as they strained to make out what else she might say.

Whoever was within didn't sound threatening. For a change, Nell didn't go with her feelings, but with her thoughts.

She looked over at Luke and said, "Let's just wait a minute till this person appears. Remember, the nicest sounding people can be bad, too."

"Okay. You get on that side of the door, and I'll stay on this side, where I can see in clearly. It's kinda dark in there!" he whispered. "Nell, grab that board down under those roses. Roses, again! This time in front! I'll go in first, if no one comes soon. You come behind me with that. Hit to hurt—smack on the head —got that?"

"Uh-huh," she said shakily, as she bent to pick up the old piece of wood that was lying pretty close to the front steps. She never once took her eyes off the door.

"Please do come in, Luke and Nell. You're causing a draft," the sweet-voiced woman from within said.

Luke and Nell looked over at each other with shocked expressions on their faces that said, 'How does she know our names?'. Now, they felt a little better thinking the person was a friend.

Luke entered hesitatingly. Nell was practically on his heels. Wherever he went she went, usually, and vice versa.

Luke almost went down for the count when he saw what was inside this beautiful little home. Nell grabbed him from behind, as he teetered a bit and stopped short.

Then, Nell saw what her brother saw and words could not describe what she was feeling.

This was not only bizarre and strange! It was beautiful and fantastic and so unreal she had to touch her face and blink her eyes and look at Luke to see if he was feeling the same thing—to see if he was still real—because she doubted she was!

There was a cozy little den-like room to their left, and, a cozy little kitchen area to their right. Both rooms were tiny.

The children didn't see much of the house on entering because of the light, the rainbow-colored glow that was coming from deeper within the small hallway.

A beautiful cocoa-brown teddy bear was approaching them. She was taller than they were and had opalescent whitish wings over her shoulders that lit up. She had a golden halo slanted diagonally on her head and one of those fuchsia-colored gorgeous pink roses higher up above the halo. Both were slanted toward her right ear.

She was carrying a huge peach-colored cat, which was frantically trying to get down out of her hands. A grayish-colored kitty was following at her heels—or, better yet, paws.

She had on a beautiful sky-blue robe, like people in choirs wore, with little silver stars all over it and silver trim on the hemline, neckline and cuffs.

She greeted them with the warmest of smiles, and said, "Well, it's about time you came in. I was beginning to get worried that you'd scurry away when you got closer to my home. But, you didn't. Congratulations!"

Nell just kept staring at her and her cats. She was beautiful! They were beautiful, too! They were Himalayans. The bigger of the two, who was now bolting behind a couch in the den, was whitish-peachy with orange tips on her ears and paws, an orange tail and an orange muzzle. And, pure light blue eyes.

The smaller cat, not by much, was a pale gray, with a deeper blue-gray face and tail. Her paws were a deeper blue-gray and her coat had a mix of paler gray—but, with a little cream color, too. Her eyes were a darker blue with a hint of gray.

Since Nell loved cats so much, she read up on all the types there were. The peachy-colored one was definitely a Flame-Point and this little bluish-gray was a Blue-Cream because of the blue with a bit of cream coloring. They were gorgeous!

Luke didn't notice the cats as much as he did this angelic teddy bear. His eyes never left her. He was mesmerized.

"Perhaps I should introduce myself. Wait just a minute—my manners are simply atrocious. Please shut the door, come in here and sit down. Don't worry about your wet shoes, water doesn't take on this floor.

Oh, and, Nell, you can leave that chunk of wood outside my door, dear."

The children did as she requested, shutting the door and moving over to the brightly-colored love seat. They sat, but not before they noticed the gleaming dome-look to the blue floor beneath their feet. It almost looked glass-like. They were afraid they might break it so they tiptoed over it. It almost looked like a sky from above.

"I know who you two are because you sent me a signal with your star-encrusted mirror I left in your hidey-hole."

"We did?" Luke asked, finally able to speak, although his mouth felt awfully dry. He didn't dare ask this bear for a drink, so he kept swallowing hard.

The bear asked if they'd like a bite to eat, or, perhaps, something to drink.

Nell answered, "That'd be great! Thank you!"

All of a sudden, out of nowhere, a dainty dish of angel-shaped cookies, with rose-colored frosting and little silver chips of candy on top appeared on the coffee table in front of them.

Two big cups of cocoa were sitting on either side of the dish. The handles of the cups were in the shape of angels—the top of the handle the angel's head—and, the gowns extended down and around, as if the angels were holding on to them.

"I thought you might be a little chilled after being out in the cold for quite awhile."

"Oh, thanks! This is super!" Luke said, with a great deal of enthusiasm, as he dug into the cookies first, despite his thirst. He thought they might disappear as quickly as they appeared.

"Now, if I may start again. I'll let you know a little about myself as you eat. When you're done, you can tell me how best I can help you. Okay?"

The children couldn't believe this was happening. They timidly munched the delicious cookies, a bit fearful of accepting food from strangers. But, she was not only a bear—she was an angel!

"My name is Hannah-Mariah Bear. I heard you guys talking about your problems, or, rather, your Guardian Angels did, and they asked me if I could come to your rescue."

"We really do have Guardian Angels?" Nell asked in awe of this Bear-Angel.

"Yes. Everybody does. They're always with you. Some people never talk to them, never ask for help. They help you anyway. And, the rest of us join in as needed."

"Wow! I know we studied about you in school. We go to a Catholic school and our teachers have spoken about angels in our Religion classes—but, it's mostly about Michael and Gabriel, you know?—all that stuff that happened thousands of years ago, way before we were born."

"Well, a lot of religions do believe in angels. But, you have a point there. Most people think of our helping people in the past. Some have a hard time believing that we're still around quite actively, mind you, today."

"Yeah. I know our Mom was reading different stories and books and I've looked at them, too. But, I've never heard of 'Bear' Angels."

"Well, you see, Nell, angels are a strange lot. We can appear in any form we want that we think will help you humans. Angels have been known to take on human form, as well as animal form. Did you know that?"

"Yes. I saw in one of those books—the stories about total strangers appearing to pick kids up before they were run over and that kind of thing. All any witnesses or the children could recall was that an ordinary person just stepped in to help and then disappeared."

"That's right! And, your Guardians felt I could help you out because my specialty is taking the form of animals. Mostly, I like to take the form of family pets—so, I can be with the owners and help them without their getting frightened. People are afraid of the unknown, you know?"

"Oh, we know!" Luke muttered, with that baffled look being replaced by one of wonder.

"You were wishing you could be animals. Is that correct?"

"Yeah," they both answered.

You gave a good list of why you'd like to be bears, right?"

"Uh-huh," Nell said, staring intently at Hannah-Mariah.

"Well, what I'd like to do to help you is this—let you become bears for awhile. You won't wear wings until it's necessary. In fact, I hardly ever wear these," she said, pointing up to hers. "And, this halo is just something else that fits the image of what an angel should look like and wear. It's not necessary."

"You can make us into bears—just like that?" Luke asked.

"Well, let's put it this way. It's something I can accomplish with a little help from my friend above and you. Do you want to try? It'll only be for awhile, but it might help you to understand some things more clearly."

"Well, if it's not gonna be forever, I can't see what it'll hurt. We'll be okay, won't we, Hannah-Mariah?" Nell queried.

"Oh, sure you will, dear!"

"Well, what do you think, Luke? Shall we become bears if angels can become bears and if they can take on human forms?"

"Why not? We're game, Hannah!" he said, after giving Nell a 'You Sure You Wanna Do This?' Look. When he saw how relaxed and unafraid she seemed, it was contagious. "Tell us what we need to do!" he said excitedly.

Chapter 6

Hannah-Mariah looked seriously at each of them. Then, she asked, "Well, remember when you found my mirror with the little stars shining on it?"

"Yes," they said in unison, with intent looks on their faces.

"Those stars appeared in the sky and reflected enough light to lead you to me, didn't they?"

The children nodded their heads up and down with awe-inspired looks on their faces.

"Well, I have a few stars left in my basket in my special Meditation Room. I have a tendency to toss them over people who look like they need help."

"If you hold onto the star in the light," she continued, "get it to reflect and think of being a bear—a small one, the size you can play with—I can do my best to get you into bear forms, smaller versions of me. The only glitch that sometimes happens is when I get you back into human forms, I'm left with those animals whose forms you took on. They become real animals, but keep a part of you."

"What part? What do you mean?" Nell asked nervously, after she looked over at Luke.

"Oh, it can be anything—a certain look, a smile, a gesture or the color of your eyes or hair or maybe even your voice. You'll be the same, but these animals will duplicate something about you. You won't lose anything."

"Oh, okay. No big deal," Luke said bravely, as he tried to look relaxed on his side of the loveseat.

"If we become bears, will we have a chance to see things from the past?" Nell asked.

"Yes! Now, if this is truly what you want, follow me."

As the two of them followed Hannah-Mariah through a dim narrow hallway, painted a sunset blue, Hannah led them to a back room on the left. The cats came along with them.

"Where'd you get the pretty kitties?" Nell asked, as they entered the semi-dark room.

"Oh, Muriel and Beatrice? They were the result of two sisters who wanted to be cats. That's why I wound up with a red-haired and a gray-haired one."

Luke and Nell were fascinated. They were thrilled. This was exciting and scary. Certainly, it was the adventure of their dreams.

Hannah-Mariah handed them each a small silver star from a pretty little basket in a corner of the room. She told them to sit on the old multi-colored braided rug and get comfy.

She knew that all the children needed was a gentle, "You can do it!" to get them to change over. She didn't want to frighten them either.

"Now, if you're really comfortable, shut your eyes for awhile and relax. When you feel completely at ease, open your eyes and look up at the ceiling."

They did as she asked. First, they stretched their legs, and, then, they closed their eyes. But, being typical kids, they were a little impatient to get on with it, so it didn't take long for them to stare at the amazing dome-shaped ceiling above them. They leaned back against the beanbags and pillows behind them.

"Now, if you're relaxed and you're looking up, focus on one of the stars up there."

The children looked at the crescent-shaped or banana-shaped moon and then at the trillions of stars. It was kind of difficult to stare at just one of them.

Hannah told them to keep their eyes on the one star they were looking at and to hold their own star, the one she had given them, in their two hands.

"Now," she said, "dream of yourselves as bears. See yourselves in bear costumes for Halloween, if you want. Just picture, and shut your eyes when you have the image in your mind."

They did as she requested and soon were dreaming dreams that they were really bears.

Hannah knew that the children had to be helped and given hope that their Dad might get better. She couldn't promise them an overnight cure, but at least she could let them see some of the reasons why things were the way they were in the Kylahy household.

In getting the two of them to focus on a star, she had gotten them into a bit of visualization.

Now, if only God would help her to let the children take on the animal bodies. He usually helped her if he thought some good would come from assuming another form.

While they were staring and looking half-asleep, she worked at changing them over. They didn't see her hold a big star on a big silver wand in front of each of them. They now had bear forms.

"Okay, children. What do you think? Are you happy with what you see?"

The two of them opened their eyes and looked at one another. They felt the fur on themselves and laughed. Nell asked Hannah-Mariah if she looked just like Luke.

Hannah handed her a mirror and said, "Take a look!"

"Wow! This is cool!" Luke said excitedly, as he glanced into the mirror Nell handed him. "Now, what do we do? We look like you, Hannah. Huh?"

"That's right, Luke. I thought if you could just feel what an animal feels, and you both wanted to be bears, you'd understand that people aren't the only ones with problems, and, maybe, you'd lose that dream of joining the Animal Kingdom and be happy to be people."

"Where do we go from here?" Nell asked, wiggling all over the rug, trying to get comfortable now that she had a little tail. It got in the way in this position.

"Would you like to go into the woods as bears?"

"Sure, let's go!" Luke answered enthusiastically, eager to get the show on the road.

"Follow me, then," Hannah said quietly, "and watch where you step."

"We need our boots. They came off when we were changed over," Luke said.

"Oh, no you don't. Bears don't need boots. We just have to be careful as we travel."

As they stepped out the front door, Nell looked at herself in it, since it was a mirror. She elbowed Luke to do the same. He grinned at himself, but felt bad that he couldn't see the grin. Usually, he liked to make faces at himself in the mirror. As a bear, he couldn't grin as big, nor see his expressions with all the fur.

"Oh, my God! This ground is freezing!" Nell exclaimed, as she walked down the front steps.

"That's right! Just a little problem for us bears to contend with."

After they followed her into the beautiful peaceful woods for awhile, they heard what sounded like a gunshot. Luke asked Hannah-Mariah whom the hunters might be shooting at. Nell quickly turned and gave him a look that said, "Who do you think? We're bears."

Luke questioned Hannah on why someone would be out there hunting now. "Isn't Hunting Season over?"

"It depends on the animals being hunted and the weapons being used, but some people are as irresponsible about hunting as they are about other things in their lives. They just don't care about anything or anybody but themselves."

"That's not right!" Nell yelled to be heard, as the other two managed to get way in front of her.

"Lots of people do things that aren't always right. Isn't that true?" Hannah-Mariah hollered back to her.

The children looked at each other, and, then, at her, as they both agreed by nodding their heads.

"We should get back nearer the house if we don't want to get shot at. Come along. Watch where you step. Look out! Nell, you almost got your foot stuck in that trap!"

"Oh, my! I never even saw it. I came so close. That's scary because I couldn't see it under the thick branches."

"That's right!" Hannah-Mariah said, as she gingerly led them back.

Luke came up close behind her and asked, "Hannah, are there traps out here set up for bears?"

"For bears and foxes and rabbits. You name the animal—someone will invent a trap to catch it with or in."

When they got back inside the cozy little cottage with the warm fire blazing and the pretty cats sitting close by, they realized that they had survived in the woods barefoot, or, rather, bare-pawed. They also didn't feel the cold, even though they had no coats on because they had the fur covering.

"Do other animals hunt you, Hannah, besides people?" Luke asked, with a mildly curious expression on his face, since he was still a bear.

"Sure they do. There aren't too many animals that are bigger than us, but there certainly are quite a few that are swifter and can jump out at us from nowhere and attack us."

"Wow! And, all the time here we thought bears had nothing to fear, huh, Luke?" Nell piped in, as the dawning of a new revelation set in.

The children sat huddled on the loveseat, talking on and on with Hannah about the dangers that lurked in the forest for bears. They weren't immune to fear.

"I thought we bears and other big animals would be so secure in our natural habitat," Luke said sadly.

"I didn't imagine anything bad could happen to such a big animal as a full-grown bear, like a trap wrapping around one or both of it's two feet," Nell added.

"Now, think about what you just said, Nell, it's 'two feet'. "

"Yeah!" Luke grinned, after Hannah's comment. "We were walkin' around out there like humans, or, bears on cartoon shows. Bears walk on all four feet. Wow! That's even more dangerous!"

"That's right!" Hannah said, as she smiled sweetly at this darling little bear. "But, where you're still wrong is the 'feet'. They're our paws."

"Luke proceeded to crack up laughing and said between giggles, "Right on, Nellie! Way to go!"

Nell looked at him and broke up laughing herself, despite her best efforts to try not to. "Hey, wait a minute, Luke! You said 'feet', too!"

Then, they both realized maybe they shouldn't be laughing and assumed a more serious demeanor. Hannah-Mariah just let them enjoy the humor in their mistake and smiled.

"Was there more you wanted us to learn about as bears, Hannah, besides the fact that the life of a bear is filled with dangers of all kinds?" Luke asked with a concerned look on his little brown furry face.

Hannah purposely avoided answering him, as she had to bide her time and take things slowly.

He was cute, too, she thought. The blue eyes on both of them were shining through their fur faces. Nell's eyes were a bright turquoise, whereas, Luke's were more of a sky-blue. They sparkled like the stars they were still holding tightly.

Another difference in the children was the fact that Nell's teeth were slightly crooked and Luke's were straight. She noticed that Luke had chewed up fingernails before he became a bear.

And, Nell had that little ponytail dangling behind, even as a bear. It was certainly unique, Hannah thought.

Chapter 7

Hannah-Mariah looked at these dear little bear-children and didn't quite know where to begin in getting them to open up about their dad's drinking problem. She found it quite amazing that they knew and understood so much.

Then, again, when you're a member of a dysfunctional family like theirs, of course you feel a lot for the person who has a problem. But, most of the time, children don't quite understand what's going on, why this horrible monster—alcohol—has such a grip on their loved ones.

Nell and Luke were really smart children. Hannah knew their teacher must've taught them something about drinking—probably, fearing that middle school students were at the age where they liked to experiment, try something at least once. And her ten or eleven year old students were potential targets of older kids.

How could she get them to understand, to have the courage to help change what they could and to "accept the things they couldn't change," as the old AA Motto went? She knew they were wise beyond their years. That's what happens to a lot of children who have problems in their families.

Some go one way and get into trouble themselves and blame their parents' drinking for what's become of them.

But, most of the kids she'd come across with alcoholic parents mature more quickly than their peers because they're dealing with problems, coping the best they can because they have to.

"You said you really wanted to solve your dad's drinking problem, if you could?" she finally asked, after contemplating how to put this.

"Definitely!" Nell said, with a determined look on her little bear face. Luke joined in with a nod and a "Yeah, we'd love to, but we don't have a clue where to begin. We've tried doing some things, but, I guess, they didn't help reach Dad."

"Like what?" Hannah asked, curious to know just how resourceful these kids were.

"Well," Nell went on for Luke, like they were thinking the same thoughts at the very same time, "when Dad buys himself those little nips and hides them, we find them and pour the stuff down the sink."

"Does he get mad at you when he finds out what you've done?" Hannah-Mariah questioned.

"Yeah!" Luke said, looking sad and dispirited. "He tells us we 'have no right to do that'. He can drink if he wants to. 'They're only little bottles.' "

"Then, we ask him why he hides it," Nell chimed in, "and he says, 'because you don't like me to drink. I love you, Darlings, yet I can't stop myself from drinking.' "

"Okay, kids. I think what you're going to have to do is take a look back at why your dad may have started drinking, what could've triggered it, and, maybe, you'll have a better understanding. I'm not promising any miracle cures because there aren't any. I wish there were!"

"As animals, you can have a certain understanding and insight that people sometimes lack. And, as bears, you do have a goodly amount of strength. You chose well when you picked an animal you wished to be! Let me give you each a pair of wings like mine. Then, pick up your stars and we'll be off. Let me place these on you. Just turn around."

As Hannah adjusted the small sets of wings onto the two children, they smiled—but looked a bit shaky.

"What's the matter? Getting cold feet, guys?" she asked as she smiled at them.

"No, no!" Luke said. "We're bears, now. Let's go wherever it is we're going. Where ARE we goin'?"

"Well, I thought we might go back a few years into your dad's past. Do you mind?"

"Oh, no, not at all," Nell answered with a questioning look, wondering how they were going to do this. "We trust you, Hannah," was all she said.

Chapter 8

"Let's go upstairs into my Observatory," she said, as her eyes sparkled like the huge star she was holding. She also had her basket of stars over her left arm.

This woman-angel-bear was so full of mystical power, she had Nell and Luke totally captivated. She was simply charming! Her voice was so melodious; they loved listening to her. Her walk was so light she almost floated. Then, again, she WAS an angel!

They followed her up 3 stairs, turned on a little landing, and, then, up 4 more. Then, they took a right.

The upstairs didn't look too big to them. In fact, it was tiny—just a couple rooms.

Hannah led them into a small back room that had all kinds of cat toys and tents. There were also carpeted trees and houses that went all over the place, stretching up to the ceiling. This was a room designed for Beatrice and Muriel, alone. Kitty Heaven! It was super! These cats had it made!

Beyond all the kitty limbs and perches and beds, the children followed Hannah to a tiny door with a mirror on it.

Nell couldn't resist asking, "Do Muriel and Beatrice like to look in the mirror to see how pretty they are?"

"Pretty? They think there are other kitties coming towards them. You should've seen the first time that Muriel walked by it. She glanced quickly, and, then, she did a double take. When she looked back again, she thought it was a big 16-pound peach-colored cat and jumped straight up in the air about 6 inches on all fours!"

The bear-children howled. They were finally feeling totally comfortable with her.

Then, Hannah-Mariah took one of the real teeny stars out of her basket and matched it up in the keyhole, which wasn't a keyhole but a star-hole.

The star lit the star-shaped hole it was placed in. A zap of opalescent color came from that particular spot and the door opened with a melody similar to the theme from Star Wars, that old movie that was currently making a return.

The kids were amazed. Luke couldn't believe what he was seeing and hearing. He thought he was in another world. He looked over at Nell, the bear—and, realized he was. Or, he soon would be.

Nell followed close on Hannah's heels and almost banged into her back when the big bear stopped shot. She banged her head a little on one of Hannah's wings. She didn't realize just how sturdy they were, since they looked so light and were almost transparent.

Hannah-Mariah quickly turned and asked if Nell was all right. When Nell said she was fine, Hannah said, "These things do sometimes become a nuisance. However, now they'll serve a good purpose for us."

The room they entered was really no more than a little landing. They had to take a sharp left near the mirrored door and climb up a spiral staircase to a semi-circular deck.

Nell thought such a place was called a 'parapet', but didn't say anything to Luke about thinking of another of their newly acquired vocabulary words.

This was Hannah's Observatory, a place from which she could gaze at the night sky and its myriad wonders—the stars, the moon, and the different planets that could be seen at certain times of the year.

"What a spot!" Luke exclaimed, with a look of pure joy on his face. "WOW!"

"Yes, it is quite nice, isn't it?" Hannah said proudly.

The children couldn't help but notice the huge telescope she had set up on its tripod off to the side.

"You can certainly see everything for miles around up here!" Nell said, totally mesmerized by what lay below them—the tree tops, the woods, the rolling hills, the squared-off fields and the houses that looked like little specks from where they were standing. "It IS a nice spot! I LOVE it!"

"Now, as bears who have wings, you'll be able to fly—once we step off this ramp out here. So, don't get nervous! Trust me. And, do as I do, okay?"

"Okay!" the children said together, thrilled to be able to do what she said they could do—FLY.

"Take your star and hold it in one hand. Come on, come out here with me," she said, as she opened an even smaller door than the one they had just come through. It was something like a Doggie Door, the way it was attached at the top.

The children were getting mixed feelings now. Although, they were excited about flying, they were also nervous and wondered if they really could. The ground was a long way down.

But, they had to trust someone. Trust was something they lacked, due to their dad's drinking problem. He made a lot of promises that he never kept. But Hannah? She hadn't steered them wrong yet. She hadn't given them a reason to not trust her.

Luke got on her left and Nell on her right.

She told them to extend the arm without the star—and, THEY DID!

She told them to close their eyes and see themselves flying—and, THEY DID!

Then, she told them to take a step—and, THEY DID!

Chapter 9

"What a fantastic way to travel!" Nell said excitedly, as she looked over at Hannah-Mariah.

"Yeah! This is great!" Luke agreed.

It was beautiful—to be up so high and to see so much. The children loved the feel of the nippy winter air in their faces.

"Where are we going, Hannah?" Luke asked when he caught up with her.

"You'll see. Be patient, Luke."

Luke tried to be patient. It was hard. He was excited. And, he was a teddy bear with angels' wings. This is unreal, he thought.

Similar thoughts were going through Nell's mind. How in the world did we get here? I can't believe this is happening! I must be dreaming!

Abruptly, they came to a stop at a drab chocolate brown house in the heart of the city. The children wondered what city it was.

"Here we are. Take a look inside this window with me. Can you see?"

"Yeah! It looks like a family and they look real sad. Who are they, Hannah?" Luke asked in a concerned voice.

"Where are we, Hannah-Mariah?" Nell piped in before Hannah got a chance to answer Luke's question.

"This is the home your dad grew up in in Haverhill, Massachusetts, right over the border from your town," she said.

"Oh, yeah. Dad pointed it out to us many times, if we happened to be riding by this way. I thought this area looked familiar!" Luke exclaimed excitedly. "Dad said it was called 'The Acre', the Irish part of the city."

"That's right. It was, Luke. Not many of the younger people who live here today realize or even care about what this area was known as. We're going to look in on your dad when he was a year younger than you are now, the age you just left today."

"There's your dad, the oldest of the three children. Those are his parents and his little sister and brother."

"But, Dad had an older brother, too—John. Where is he?" Nell asked, with trepidation in her voice.

"Listen," Hannah whispered and put her index finger to her lips, signaling them to keep quiet.

"It's all my fault. If I hadn't gone to the show with my cousin, my brother would still be alive! I should've stayed with him!"

"Michael, Michael, how can you say such a thing?" his father asked him, as he looked at his son with concern and sadness.

The parents were devastated by the death of their oldest son, it was apparent.

"John would have probably crossed Franklin Street at that same moment, whether or not you were with him. In fact, you may have been killed, too."

"Dad, don't you see? John and Pete had an argument. Pete asked me to come with him to the show—and, like a fool, I went. I should never have left my brother! I feel so bad! It's all my fault! That drunk guy wouldn't have hit John if I were with him, because John wouldn't have been crossing the street. We'd've gone in the back yard and played or gone down by Little River, the other way. Oh, what have I done?" he sobbed uncontrollably.

His mother was in a fog. She just looked dazed. She wasn't saying anything. Puppy was trying to calm their dad down, but it didn't seem to be working.

Luke looked over at Hannah and said in a hushed tone, "Gee, we knew Uncle John was killed by a drunk driver, but we never knew that Dad felt it was his fault."

"Where did it happen, Hannah—down the street?" Nell asked, with tears in her eyes.

"Oh, no. Right here. Right in front of their house. And, the saddest part was—your dad came home, while he lay dying. The emergency technicians knew they couldn't help him."

"Oh, that's horrible! Poor Daddy! And, the guilt he must've felt in leavin' him like that. But, Daddy wasn't involved in the argument from what I remember him tellin' us the few times he talked about it," Nell said.

"No, he wasn't—but, he always blamed himself for siding with his cousin all through the rest of his childhood and into his teen years. He missed him something awful. John was only two years older than he was."

"He felt he should be the 'man of the house' after John's death because your grandfather worked long hours at the shoe factory."

"He'd run home from school each day at lunch time to check on his mother, since the school was only a few blocks away."

"He was worried about her. She didn't pay much attention to him or his little sister, your Aunt Leonore. She gave all of her attention to his baby brother, Patrick. She went to the cemetery every day to visit John's grave. She was a basket case, or as you guys would say, "Nutso". Your dad thought she was going to die. She was never the same afterward. He and your aunt never got much warmth and love from her. It was his dad, your 'Puppy', who watched over them.

"Wow! This had to have an effect on Dad throughout his life, didn't it Hannah?" Luke asked.

"It sure did, Luke! When someone feels guilt and a lot of sadness, they sometimes try to run from it, to hide from it. It's a terrible thing! And, he- a nine-year-old—shouldn't have felt this. What made matters worse was that his mother didn't go on living her life for her living children. She lived it, dwelling on the child she lost. Sure, it was terrible! It was sad. But your dad and Auntie Leonore needed her. They were hurting, too. He was their big brother!" Hannah said almost vehemently.

"A lot of mothers, a generation or two ago, loaded their sons with guilt trips, so they wouldn't leave them and get married. She did that with him, too, later on. She even tried to get him to talk your aunt out of getting married—or, at least, to postpone it—after your grandfather had a heart attack."

Hannah-Mariah had never spoken in such an angry tone before now.

"Have you two seen enough of this?" she asked.

"Yes, we have. Please take us away from Franklin Street and the Acre, Hannah," Nell begged.

Chapter

They held their stars and spread their arms again, and followed her across the city to a more rural setting on the west side of Haverhill—Riverview Drive.

"Oh, I know where we are now," Luke said happily. "This is where Ma and Dad lived when they were first married."

"You're right, Luke. You do recognize the pretty house your Lithuanian grandfather built. He left it to your parents because they moved in to take care of him when he was bed-ridden with cancer. Your Uncle Joe promised him that he'd take care of Nanny when she couldn't take care of herself. As it turned out, your parents lived there a little while with her after he died—but, they sold it when she didn't want to live there anymore on her own because of the memories."

"I remember it, too. We used to come here and visit when we were real little," Nell said, with a nostalgic dreamy look in her eyes.

"Well, let's climb onto the nice closed-in front porch and take a peek inside, shall we?"

"Okay, Hannah. Nothing can be as bad as Dad's childhood," Luke said sadly.

"This isn't pretty, believe me," Hannah said, as she leaned in to look at the scene transpiring in the pretty white-walled room with natural wood trim around the windows and doors.

The children followed her lead and peered in, too. They saw a younger version of their mother and father. They looked to be in their early twenties. Ma was sitting on a beautiful rattan couch, with pretty bright pink floral cushions. Dad was on the matching chair near the window, smoking away.

"Hey, Nell, that's the set Ma has in the Reading Room, now—only it's painted black and the cushions are a red and blue plaid."
"Yeah, Luke. I recognize it!"
"Shhh!" Hannah-Mariah whispered, as she pointed her finger toward the window to show them there was talking going on inside.

"I tell you, Mary. It was really bad! What I saw over there—it blew my mind!"
"I know Mike. It bothered you a lot, but you have to get on with your life—our life."

The kids remembered Dad saying he was in the Gulf War—but he never talked about it in depth. They looked at Hannah, as she pointed to something in the room.
"Look what's on the table beside your dad," she said.

They watched him start talking again. He was pretty shaky. He took another puff of the cigarette in the ashtray beside him — and, then, he gulped a drink.
"They called it 'Friendly Fire', Mary, 'Friendly Fire'! My buddies, Mac and Ron, getting shot down by our own planes! Can you believe that? You don't

know how close I came to 'biting the dust'! You can't imagine!"

"I know it was rough, Mike! I feel bad for you. I know it'll take time to get over it—but you will. Meanwhile, I do think you should try to get back on your feet and go back to work. They won't hold your job open for you much longer. And, dear, it'd be good for you to be with people and get your mind on something else."

"I'll go when I get around to it." He took another guzzle of his drink, and, then, puffed the cigarette again.

"Michael, you've been back from the war for 4 months, now. Your boss said he'd keep the job open for you for 6. Are you planning on waiting that long? The longer you stay home, the more you're dwelling on the war. And, that's not good for you!"

"Yeah, yeah, I know! Get off my back, will you? I need a little time to unwind, relax, ya know?"

"If we could afford for you to stay home—fine! But, we can't, Honey. And, I'm really worried about all this drinking. You weren't drinking like this before you went over and you didn't smoke either. Besides, you're starting to get belligerent—you're always on the defensive."

"Well, Darly, being involved in a war will do a lot of things to people. My nerves are a bit shattered and these things help. I'm sorry I was a little nasty with you."

"What do they do—hide the fact that you were there? Blot out the memory? You can't do that, Mike. Time is a healer. If you need help to deal with your psychological problems—go for it! I'll go with you, if you want. I just don't want to see you get hooked on this stuff!"

"Don't worry, Hon, it's only temporary. I can stop whenever I want."

The children watched their mother leave the room, fighting back tears. Their father didn't even notice the state she was in because he was off in a drunken little stupor of his own.

"Was this when Dad got into drinking, Hannah?" Luke asked with unshed tears, waiting to fall from his baby blue eyes.

"Yes. He used to have an occasional drink with your mother when they'd eat out or celebrate a holiday, but nothing big deal. It was just something you did."

"When he returned from the war, he could no longer handle it like he thought he could. He eventually lost this job because he never went back in the allotted time span. And, he lost a few more jobs, while you kids were little."

"That's why your mother went from working part-time to full-time. He wasn't a steady jobholder. The alcohol had such a hold on him that he couldn't just stop when he wanted to."

"He became addicted to cigarettes, too, for a time, but when your mom learned she was pregnant with you, she asked him to give those up for your sakes. She knew how bad second-hand smoke was for pregnant woman and the children they were carrying. She didn't know, yet, that there were two of you. So, he did manage to at least give up the ciggies, for the most part, maybe, because he never was a smoker before all this happened."

"Thank God for that!" Nell said. "Not too many people smoke today, do they? It's almost as if they're made to feel like outcastes—the way they have the 'NO

SMOKING' signs in buildings. I've seen some people standing outside of work places with cigarettes, but it's like that's the only place they can go now."

"Yeah," Luke said. "I've seen some of the old-fashioned classic movies, and they all smoked. It was the 'cool' thing to do back then. Those poor people didn't know how addictive or how harmful nicotine was for them. That's so sad!"

"It certainly is, Luke! You know a whole lot about the bad effects of cigarettes," Hannah-Mariah said, with a look of amazement that he knew so much and felt so strongly.

"What some people can't understand is that those who are addicted to alcohol and nicotine find it almost impossible to give them both up. A lot of recovering alcoholics keep smoking because they feel it helps ease the edginess that accompanies giving up the liquor. Because your dad doesn't smoke anymore, he's having a problem with giving up the alcohol all the time."

"It's gotta be so hard for him. Are we through with our visit here, Hannah? I feel so bad for both Ma and Dad! Wars are rough and they do change people, 'psychologically'—how's that one, Luke—as well as, physically. Some people's hurts are so deep; they don't let others know. Do they, Hannah?"

"That's true, Nell. You're right about emotions and the mind playing a big role in affecting our soldiers. Sometimes, it's more difficult to live with our thoughts than it is with the physical scars. And, you're right, Nell, nobody knows. Are you about ready to leave Riverview Drive? We have a third stop to make."

"Yes. Let's go, Hannah. I'm not looking forward to it, but I understand why you're having us make these visits," Luke resignedly said, as he faced Hannah-Mariah.

Chapter 11

The children followed Hannah through the air like old pros at this flying business. They were enjoying the feel of the breezes and the fantastic views that they got from up on high. They weren't as happy with the visits they had to make.

"We're coming to our third and final stop now. So, gently slow down. Here we are!"

"This looks like the place Dad works, Hannah. Is it?" Nell asked.

"Yes. We'll have to land on this balcony outside his boss' office. Just don't look down, if you don't like heights," she said humorously.

They laughed as they carefully landed. Luke responded, "If either of us had any fear of heights before today, I think we've lost it by now, Hannah."

"I guess you have. It's just that some people like to be moving on high, but get a little nervous when they're standing still up high—like out here. It's not the fear of heights, but a fear of open spaces."

"I know what you mean, Hannah. Our school building is an old one that has a fire escape stairway coming down the outside from the third floor. Some kids used to get real shaky on those open stairs, where you can see right through. They said they felt like they were going to fall through," Nell mentioned. "I felt that way, myself, a couple of times."

"You hit it on target, Nell. That's a perfect example!" Hannah said, with an amazed look on her face at the brightness of these two kids. "Okay, now, let's take a peek. Not much of the blind is open, but it's enough for us to see a little."

As Nell and Luke leaned over one another and Hannah leaned above them, they could see into the large corporate office. There was a dark mahogany desk, with huge floor-to-ceiling bookshelves extending the length of the wall behind it. They could see a man at the desk.

"That's Mr. Monhegan, Dad's boss, Nell. Remember, we met him at that Employee Party he threw last summer?"

"Yeah, the one where there were all kinds of contests and everyone was supposed to let him win because it was his house and he was the boss. Dad could've won a lot of those, like riding the tricycles, but he let Mr. M. win because it was the 'right' thing to do."

"I know you and I got mad at him for holding back. Ma went right along with him, like it was all in fun. What kind of fun is that when you give up a win you rightly could have? I don't get it!"

"Well, Luke, that's just one of the ways your father and the people he works with feel—that they have to go along. You keep the boss happy at all costs, even if you know it isn't right and you don't feel comfortable with it. You 'play the game'," Hannah explained. Now, pay attention and let's see what's going on in here."

The children watched Mr. Monhegan's face and heard him say, "Now, Mike. You know I don't want to let you go. But, if you keep going on these little drinking binges and needing time to dry out—I'll have to. The other guys in your department can only cover for you for so long. Do you understand?"

"But, Fred. I don't do it often. Working for this company hasn't helped my drinking habit, you know? You do throw parties and encourage us to drink. You have us out to eat and it's expected of us to drink. Hey, even when I go away to dry out and come back with a new resolve to drink no more, guys who are supposed to be my friends say things like, 'Come on Mike. It's Friday. Just come out and have one drink before you go home. What harm is a little drink gonna do you?' "

"You don't have to go," Mr. M. said smugly. "No one's twisting your arm."

"Oh, come on, Fred! The pressure here is tremendous to join in and not be a 'Party Pooper'. When my work on these computers suffers, I'm told someone else'll take over. I'm made to feel I'm dispensable, which I know I am. Hey, I put in seven good years here. Sure, I've taken a little time off. I just wish certain people would stop putting pressure on me to drink!"

"Well said, Mike! And, I do understand for you. I don't know how to tell people to leave you alone. That's something you'll have to do yourself. Others can hold their liquor and—"

"Now, wait just a minute! I'll be the first to admit I may have a hard time stopping, once I get started. But, I don't need fellow-employees getting me going either. I think, if they really cared for me, they wouldn't do what they do."

"Well, Mike. I don't know what to say. I'll give you one more chance. I've given you so many. Don't blow it. This is it! You either get a handle on this problem—or, you ship out—plain and simple. You're very good at the work you do—but I can get steadier people to do what you're doing and start them at less money. You can go back now."

The twins heard their dad get up and walk with a steady gait toward the door on the left. As they bent to peek in further, they caught a quick glance of the upset look he shot at Mr. Monhegan before he firmly shut it.

"Do you see another reason for your dad's drinking, Nell and Luke?" Hannah asked with a very concerned and empathetic look on her pretty bear face.

"Yes. It's the pressure thing again—like Nell and I were saying earlier. Kids aren't the only ones who have to deal with peer pressure. Grown-ups do, too. It's out there in the workplace, no matter where people work."

"You know what really bothers me, Hannah?" Nell joined in with a mad look on her face. "If people really cared for you, they wouldn't do this type of thing. You know, just like kids at school, so-called 'friends' that get their buddies into smoking or drinking or drugs. What is it? Are they afraid to try things alone? Or, are they jealous of those who don't need that stuff to be happy? Some people and kids can deal with their problems and really learn to cope without becoming dependent on a chemical. And what happens when they're not drinking or whatever? They can't deal with reality. The real world's still there, but they can't face it. That's pretty sad!"

"You're a hundred percent right, Nell, and I only wish a lot of adults out there were as wise as you two. Sometimes, they're so enmeshed in their own problems. Sometimes, they don't mean to hurt people. But, a lot of them do. There are mean people and mean kids. It's a fact of life."

"Yeah, and by the look of it, Dad seems to be on shaky grounds with this boss and company. I didn't know he'd dare to talk to Mr. Monhegan this way. I'm proud of him!" Luke said with a big smile.

"You should be, Luke. He's fighting the good fight. But, sometimes trying to come up against a whole lot of people who think the same way about things is difficult. If no other people there feel the same way, if none of the others have the same problem he has, he isn't going to get them to change."

"I wondered where he'd go for a few days at a time or for a week," Nell said. Ma never told us he was at a drying-out place, trying to get the alcohol out of his system. She said it was for his job."

"I'm sure she didn't want to worry you kids. Your dad does seem to be realizing he has a problem. He just won't admit it to any of you. Admitting you have a problem, is the first step for an alcoholic. Until they can do this, nobody can help them. They have to want the help or someone's good intentions are all to no avail. He'll have people tuned out."

"Gee, it almost looks like there's hope for Dad— like, maybe, even if he got another job with more understanding people, he'd have a chance to be okay," Luke said, with a guarded optimism.

"Coming from Luke, this is a change!" Nell said to Hannah. "He's usually the pessimist and doesn't see any bright lights at the end of the tunnels."

"Well, that's great! Never give up on your dad, Luke! You're right, there certainly is hope! He needs your support and encouragement just as much as you children need his. Don't let him down. Be there for him. Show him you understand what he must be going through at work. Even if you can get him to open up and talk about those pressures with you, it'd be of help to him. Remember that alcoholism is a disease. His drinking is not his fault. And, he is not a 'drunk.' This derogatory name is used by people who don't know any better. They don't have a clue about this illness."

"We know, Hannah," Nell responded, "and, don't worry about us trying to help Dad. We'll keep at it. Right, Luke?"

"We sure will!" Luke agreed, with an encouraging look on his teddy bear face.

"I believe you!" Hannah smilingly exclaimed. "We have to be getting back now, so you can change over and head home. Your parents have a search party out looking for you," she added very carefully, so as not to get them anxious. "They just started looking. Your disappearance will be short-lived. Are you ready to fly?"

"Yes!" they both said with gusto, realizing this'd be their last chance at it and knowing they'd be going back to their parents with a little more understanding of the roots of their dad's sickness. They now had renewed optimism that they could help and were eager to return.

Chapter 12

Enjoying this flight immensely, the children tried to take in all that they saw between their father's workplace in Norwood, Massachusetts and their pretty colonial home in Atkinson. They passed over several big highways and watched the cars travelling along at a slow crawl.

Lots of people were heading into Boston for 'First Night' Celebrations. Any traffic going in the direction they were flying was lighter because there weren't as many places to 'Ring in the New Year' on New Year's Eve north of Boston as there were in the big city.

Some people were going to company parties that weren't as ostentatious.

Nell and Luke knew their parents would be worried now because this was the time they, too, would be heading out to party, if their children hadn't disappeared on them.

Oh, are we gonna get it, was the thought on both of their minds, as they landed on the little ramp behind Hannah and quickly ducked through the teeny door into her Observatory.

Hannah helped them take off their wings and hurried them down to the Meditation Room. In here, she asked them to calm down, though this was now difficult after what they'd been through, and to start visualizing again.

So, holding their stars and shutting their eyes, they tried to focus on what she was saying and see themselves as people again, as children, and not bears, bear-children. It took a little longer to transfer back to human form because they were experiencing contradictory feelings—being tense and nervous on the one hand—and, excited and optimistic on the other.

* * *

Meanwhile, back at their home, their parents were going frantic. It wasn't until a couple hours after the children left that their mother started to get concerned.

She knew that the children loved to go into the woods and play, pretending they were animals because once she went looking for them when they weren't around. She saw them carefully going over a little stream and didn't want to interfere with their fun. She was a kid once herself, and enjoyed doing the same things. She knew that stream wasn't deep, the children were sensible and they were good swimmers. She knew they couldn't drown in that water unless they were laying down face first. And, that wouldn't happen because they had each other. She'd never let one go out there exploring alone.

So, she let them be for a couple hours before she allowed her concern to come to the surface. She told Mike when he asked about them, as he entered the tomb-like house. It was never this quiet.

He worked until three and scurried home to get ready for the party.

"Mike, I'm sure they're all right. I was just worried about feeding them, having their birthday party and then getting ready for your company party later, so I thought I'd go and yell to them. I probably should've called them sooner, but I know how they love to play back there.

Mike paced back and forth like a nervous wreck. He never looked so scared in his life.

Mary tried to reassure him. "Look, I'll give Len and Tom a call, and maybe they can come over earlier than they planned, if they have the time. That way the four of us can go out together."

All Leonore needed was Mary's somewhat shaky voice on the phone. She explained where the kids were headed and that she wasn't worried, but Mike was. Mary knew Mike's sister, who loved Nell and Luke as if they were her own, would want to help them if she could.

"We're on our way. We'll be there in 15 minutes. Wait for us please, Mary. Okay?"

"All right," Mary said, as calmly as she could. She told Mike they were coming and added, "So, why don't we change over into something warm while we wait?"

Mike tried to calm a bit, but he couldn't. All he could think of was his babies out there in the cold woods, playing around near that stream.

Mary told him it wasn't that deep. "I bet they're having such a great time, they don't have any concept that it's been a couple of hours. They don't have watches, so they really don't have a clue what time it is when they go out there, you know."

"Oh, Mary! I'd die if anything happened to them! I love them so much! Sometimes, I don't get a chance to show them, but you know I do! Just like I couldn't go on without you."

"I know and so don't Nell and Luke. They love you, too, Mike!"

"Yeah, but I know I upset them a lot with my drinking. They get mad at me and want me to quit. They begged me, but I said, 'Oh, no, I can't. What would my boss think? What about my image as a worker who gets along well?'"

"I have been so dumb, Mar! Why haven't I realized what was most important to me in my life? Why haven't I got my priorities straight? Oh, dear God, what'll I do if anything happens to them?"

"Look, Mike, we'll be out there looking with Len and Tom in five minutes. Meanwhile, why don't we gather all the flashlights we can find. I'll make a pot of coffee and fill a couple of thermoses. You go and put on some warmer clothes and your boots because it's kind of mucky out there. Lenny and Tom will be here, soon. I'll get my boots on. Do you want me to call the police, or do you want to look on our own first?" All the time she talked to him she tried so hard to not let her fears for the children show. She didn't want to get him more upset.

"If you're sure they're okay, why don't we four take a look first? If, after a little while, we can't find them, I'm sure we can get Dutch and Tony over here quickly. They're not party animals. I doubt Atkinson's finest is doing the 'Drinking Party Connection' tonight, not like this very selfish father. Where have I been?"

"Let's head out back. I think I see Tom's Bronco comin' up the hill. Yeah, there they are! Let's go!"

Chapter 13

Lenny and Tom came hurrying into the driveway at a quick clip. They jumped out of their four-wheel drive vehicle and ran to hug Mary and Mike.

Len immediately asked if they were all right. She looked concernedly at her brother and saw the tears that were surfacing in his eyes.

"All right, you know where they like to play out here, Mar, so lead the way. Here, Tom, here's a flashlight for you, too, Hon," she said to her husband as she grabbed the lights her sister-in-law handed her.

Tom, a quiet serious man, was the opposite of Lenny as far as personality went. She was more the talker, the vivacious one. He took it and followed Mary through the woods that were just starting to get a little dark and eerie.

Lenny stayed behind to grab Mike's arm and tell him, "Don't worry, Mike. I'm sure they're fine. They just lost track of the time. You know how distracted those two can get."

"I know. It's just that I love them so much, Len. I've been blind 'til now. I've been so wrapped up in my work and all that goes on there, thinking I'm supposed to keep up the image like the big shots. Drink—Party — or else, I'll lose my job. I won't fit in. They'll think I'm 'not cool'! Boy, where have I been? My drinking always bothered them and I just never heard them when they complained—oh, what I mean is I heard—

but I didn't bother to listen. Oh, to have the chance to listen to their little voices again!"

"Michael, don't you ever get maudlin on me. This is your sister, who happens to love you! Yeah, you have been kind of a jerk about not payin' attention to them, but we'll find them and remedy the situation. Okay? You'll now be able to really give them your ears. All right? Trust me, they're out there playing. They're smart kids like their dad."

He laughed and hugged his little sister. "You know you're a pretty sharp little girl, yourself, Len? I'm so lucky to have you for a sister! All I think of is when we lost John. I couldn't go through something like that again!"

"Oh, here we go, another 'Irish Guilt Trip'. Come on, Mikey! Why are you blaming yourself because they're out in these woods?"

"It isn't because they went here, but why? If I'd been a better Daddy to them, if I didn't touch a drop, they wouldn't need to go out into the woods and run away from their troubles."

"Come on, Michael Jude! Give yourself a break! The kids like to play out here. Period. They're not running away from their troubles, they're doing what kids do—looking for adventure, dreaming of being Robin Hood in Sherwood Forest. Who knows what they're imagining! But, it's good for them to have time alone from grown-ups, too, you know, especially their parents. They don't know what you guys will think of their fantasies. They can be freer to let loose and express themselves outside than they can in the house. Wouldn't you have just loved all this land when we were little, Mikey? I know I would've."

"Yeah. We had fun, though, in the city. We used our imaginations."

"That's true, we did. But, Ma wouldn't let any of us far from her sight, after John's death."

"You know, Lenny, I still miss him. I wonder what kind of man he would've been. I—"

"Don't you dare say you blame yourself, Mike. You were a little kid. They had the argument. If you were dear Cousin Pete—all right. But, you were the youngest and you just went with him because he was going to buy you goodies at the show. Whoopee! No one knew John would cross the street at that time."

"I know, Baby Sister. I realize that now. And, thanks for making me see it, after all these years. Ma didn't do you or me any favors in alleviating our guilt, did she?"

"No. Remember, she asked you to talk to me about postponing my wedding plans because Dad was sick?"

"Yeah, and I told her, 'No Way!' Dad told me on the side, she just wanted to hold onto you, so she wouldn't have to start caring and feeling again. Your getting married and leaving her to be responsible for Dad's care was the best thing that could've happened to her. It helped take her mind off John, somewhat, I think."

"I do, too. Now, let's help Tom and Mar find those darling children of ours, shall we? I hear them hollering their lungs out."

Mike looked a lot less tense after talking to his sister all the way out to the stream. He felt happy when he heard Lenny refer to his kids as 'our' kids, which meant she and Tom loved them like he and Mary did!

Leonore and Tom couldn't have kids even though they wanted several. That's always the way it works, he thought. People who want kids, love them and would make good parents never have kids. Then, there are those people who should've never had them. They don't appreciate the joys children can bring. Some are neglectful and abusive.

Two kids were never wanted more than my two. "Oh, please let them be safe, dear God," he said silently, as he trudged along the streambed, following the others.

"This is where I've seen them jump across these big fat rocks and cross to the other side," Mary yelled. "I think we can get across without jumping over them, if we follow the stream down a little ways."

"Okay. Let's go!" said Tom, as he led the way to the right. "It narrows down well enough here that we can just hop across. Come on folks!"

Mary and Lenny hurried up behind him, with Mike following up the rear. He kept looking at the stream, wondering how deep it was, since he never took the time to come out here. He was looking into the water to see brightly-colored clothing beneath the surface. "Please, dear God, let them be okay," he kept saying. It was his mantra.

The four of them made it over and spread out a little, but within sight of one another, then started up the shore, flashing their lights on the ground in front of them, beside them and ahead of them.

Chapter 14

Suddenly, Len stopped dead in her tracks and yelled to the others, "What's that over there? It looks like a little building—a hut, maybe?"

"Yeah, it does, Lenny! Let's go take a look. That's the type of place I can see Nell and Luke hiding in, or maybe even putting together themselves," Mary said.

"Nell! Luke!" Mike yelled out, as the four of them approached it. Tom did the same. No answer.

The woods were silent, except for an occasional tweeting of a bird who made his home out here.

Mary ran to catch up with Lenny, since Lenny was the closest and approaching it quickly. Len just wanted to make it to them before their parents, just in case.

She arrived and peeked inside. Then, she went in and hardly had time to notice the little blackboard and shelf that were set up in a dingy corner before Mary stepped in. She quickly stood in front of the blackboard, so Mary wouldn't see what she had discovered.

However, Mar knew her sister-in-law too well and noticed the abrupt move to the left. "What are you hiding behind you, Leonore? Come on. Let me see."

Lenny didn't know what to do or say, so she let Mar see what was on the board.

As Mary got up close to it and started to read it, Mike and Tom came in, crouching to fit through the opening that was meant for kids only.

Len and Mary didn't have a problem coming through, as they were both thin women of average height. They merely had to bend a bit at the waist. The men were a lot bigger. They were both broad-shouldered; and, Mike was a foot taller than Mary.

Now, Tom and Mike spotted the blackboard, too. They sat on the pieces of logs the kids had used as chairs. Mike almost fell off of his when he saw what they had written on the old board. It was a list of "New Year's Resolutions On How We Can Help Dad With His Drinking Problem."

On the left were the problems as they saw them, and on the right were the ways they planned on resolving them:

Problem	Resolution
1 When Dad says he has to go out	1 Take the keys, don't let him get them, hide them
2 When Dad brings home liquor & keeps hiding it in the cellar ceiling rafters	2 Keep ditching it, but do it in front of him, let him get mad

3 When Dad shouts & swears at Ma & us after he's been to a party on Friday night	3 Take Ma & the keys to the truck & go out, put him to bed —No, he could burn the house down cuz sometimes he sniggles ciggies home on Fridays, so just ignore him???
4 If Dad ever says, "I need help!"	4 Get him to an AA Meeting fast! Yeah!

He had to laugh at this last one's remedy. But, it didn't last long because he was crying so hard. The others comforted him.

"Oh, what can I do to make it all up to them?" he asked no one in particular. "Dear God and St. Christopher, even though you got kicked off the Saints' List, you help people traveling. Please guide them. And, St. Anthony, dear 'Saint of Things That Are Lost', please help me find my precious babies. I'll make ONE New Year's Resolution right now in front of the three of you. If God finds a way to give me back my kids, I'll never touch another drop of liquor. This is something they want. They knew I had a problem before I did. Dear God, please bring them home to me so I can tell them how smart they are!"

The others were in tears with him now. Tom and Len were so distraught—consoling him, hugging Mary, and all of them crying on each other's shoulders—that they didn't hear the voices coming through the woods.

"Bye-Bye, Hannah-Mariah. We'll miss you!" the children said as they waved to her and the bluebird on her shoulder. They watched her, as she disappeared back into the thick dark woods. They could see that opalescent light that surrounded her for awhile. She disappeared. Then, the light did.

While they were on their way to the shore on the far side, their father and mother and aunt and uncle crossed the water down below, where it was narrow. The four of them were so grief-stricken that they had to sit near the water's edge, and think about what they'd do now. They wondered if they should get the police involved as they sat in a stupor, four lost and heart-broken souls.

As they sat there hugging one another, Tom happened to glance up and thought he saw two little streams of light, shining dimly, directly across from them. He didn't say anything to the others, at first, because he thought it was his imagination playing tricks on him or wishful thinking. Then, he looked again and saw that the glow, almost the color of reflected opals, was getting a little brighter.

So, he said, "Don't get excited and don't say anything—but, do you see what I see over there across the stream?"

The others were dumbfounded and hesitant to call out, so they just sat there staring.

They heard a determined young boy's voice saying, "I'll go first!"

"No, I will!" a girl's voice returned.

"I must lead to show you I'm not afraid, Nell!"

The children didn't see the grown-ups yet. When the four of them heard Nell and Luke talking, their hearts started pounding and they jumped up excitedly.

Mary was the first to yell, "Nellie! Luke! Are you over there? Is that you, Darlings?"

"Yeah, Ma! It's us! Are you really mad?" Nell answered, looking happy but scared because it was late.

"Dad? Uncle Tom and Auntie Lenny? You're there, too?" Luke yelled across, as he joined Nell at the water's edge.

"Of course, we're here, Son. We've been worried stiff over you guys. Now, come across real carefully, you hear?"

"You're not angry, Daddy? You're probably missing your party right now all because of us. It's our fault you'll be late!" Nell hollered.

"Just come over here, please. You have nothing to worry about ever again. Daddy's not going to the darn party. He could care less. How do you like that?" their father yelled back.

The kids couldn't jump over the rocks in the stream quick enough. As Luke jumped one at a time, Nell would jump the one he just left and tell him to hurry up.

Their mother said, "Take it easy! Go slowly! There's no rush, Darlings. We're not going anywhere."

Once they jumped all the way over to the side their parents were on like little frogs, they landed in four sets of arms. Ma and Uncle Tom hugged Nell, while Dad held Luke in his grip with Auntie Leonore grabbing both of them. Then, they switched huggers.

The children were thrilled. So were their parents and aunt and uncle. They just hugged and kissed for the longest time.

When Nell glanced down, as she was being passed back and forth, she noticed the stars that Hannah insisted they keep, on the ground near their feet. She didn't want Ma and Dad to wonder what they were and ask all kinds of questions they couldn't answer right now, so she gently kicked them behind a log nestled against a big boulder. They could come back for them later. The stars would be safe for now.

Their folks told them about discovering their clubhouse and their list of resolutions.

Nell and Luke started to lower their heads because they figured what they wrote probably hurt their dad's feelings. But, he said, "Look at me, you two!"

They raised their faces to him. God, I'm so lucky! he thought, as he looked at his little angels. (If he only knew!) "Don't feel bad about the list. You kids have been nothing but honest with me all along. I was just too blind to see that I was an alcoholic. And, of course, I didn't wanna hear it from my own kids. I want you to know, though, that I have been tryin' to fight my boss and the people at work, but it's so hard!"

"We know, Dad," Luke said, as he looked at his father proudly and gave him a hug.

"You do?" his father asked.

"Well, what I mean is we kinda figured you did," realizing his blunder. They mustn't let their father know they saw him at work.

"Oh, well, I just want to tell you that fearing for your lives got my priorities straight now. I realize how much you mean to me, how much I love you and I'm making the same resolution in front of you two that I did in front of Ma and Auntie Lenny and Uncle Tom awhile ago—that I'll never touch another drop. I promised God, too. I told him if you came back to me safe and sound, I'd do that! And, here you are! You can help me. But, you won't have to hide bottles because they'll never again be any—no anger and swearin', well, maybe, an occasional family squabble—but, it won't be because I'm drunk. And, yes, the four of us can take in some AA Meetings. I'll even speak at them, if you'd like, someday. How's that?"

"Cool, Dad!" Luke said with moist eyes. Nell was trying her hardest to smile and not cry, too. They hugged him and each of them grabbed an arm, excitedly, as they all started walking back towards their home.

Their mother fell behind and noticed something shiny and silvery glittering from under a log behind a huge rock. She had seen Nell kick at these things earlier. She wondered what they were. She didn't say anything. Maybe, someday, the children would tell her what they were.

For now, she was content that they were back and they were safe and with their Daddy—a Daddy, who wouldn't be going to New Year's Parties ever again, she hoped and prayed.

Chapter 15

Six Months Later

Mike Kylahy sipped his morning cup of Bokar Coffee, as he looked out the window and watched Luke and Nell hightailing it into the woods. He really didn't mind the fact they went there often. He understood. Kids needed time alone.

They had been playing in their huge backyard. He could hear their laughter and he could hear Mar's sweet voice chiming in. She was out there checking on her tomato plants.

Life was good for him. Boy, had it turned around!

The design work he used to do for his old company, he now did at home. Only he didn't work for that company any more and he didn't do the same type of work.

Mary and he talked about ways in which he could avoid the booze and agreed that the only place people egged him on to drink was at the office. If he left—end of problem, hopefully.

The difficult thing with leaving was the fact that he had no other job prospects. Mary said, "It's okay. I do. I finally got offered a Counseling position in the public school I've applied to. Now, I'll be making twice the money and get benefits I never got at St. Andrew's."

"That's great, Sweetheart!" he said enthusiastically, as he jumped up and hugged her. "I'm so happy for you! But, Mar, I don't think we can swing things on just your pay until I find something."

"Michael Jude Kylahy, do you have any idea what a smart and talented guy you are? It wouldn't be difficult to set you up with your own office, right in this house. Heaven knows, we have enough rooms!"

"You know you're right, Mar. I've toyed with the idea of working from home for years, but I've been working so hard I haven't had the chance to do more than that."

"Sure, you can do your design work right from our study upstairs. We can move things around, get you a bigger desk, some file cabinets and you can design!"

"Wouldn't it be great! Do you really think I can do it, Mar?"

"Why would I think otherwise? Mike, just think of it, in between your work you can go down and eat, sit outside and take a break in the nice weather. You'd make your own hours. If you'd rather work in the mornings and evenings and take the afternoons off, you can!"

"Gee, Mar, this sounds great! I've always wanted to illustrate children's books. I'd love to write them, too! You know how much I love English! Look at our poor kids—they're walking dictionaries, between their teacher's and my prodding them to look up words all the time."

"Of course you can do it! I'd even help you with some of the things little kids like. Remember, I taught Second Graders for many years."

"That'd be great, Mar! We could work together when you have the time, that is!"

"Mike, Counseling is a job that doesn't require a lot of "home" work. It does involve more time after school seeing kids and their parents, but no correcting and making up of tests and all that stuff."

This was how the dream job came about. For five months now, he was writing and illustrating not only kids' books, but also games for kids and the graphics for computer games. He'd get in touch with different companies and collaborate with the person who thought up the game. He thought up some himself, too. A whole new world was opening up to him.

As far as the drinking went, he hadn't touched a drop since before New Year's. He stuck to his resolution. It was hard, at times, because the craving used to come when he first started out working on his own.

Mary didn't understand that he still worried about bringing in the money. It took awhile. It wasn't until he started getting paid for some of his work that he could relax.

The whole family was really good about abstaining from liquor when he was with them. Lenny and Tom were a Godsend! They'd have a pot of coffee brewing or ice coffee in the fridge, depending on the season. He loved the ice coffee.

He also had these two beautiful stray cats that soon became indoor pets to pamper in between his work. He'd take a break and enjoy their company. They always helped him to relax. They always purred. It was like they were constantly talking to him.

He honestly didn't know where they came from. He did remember Luke and Nell telling some story about how these two cats just happened to follow them home from the school bus stop one day. He didn't believe it for an instant.

First of all, they were Purebred Himalayans! They were beautiful! Luke and Nell seemed to have picked out names for them as soon as they arrived. The kids also explained to him that they weren't lost or strays, that they were their guardians. "Don't worry, Dad," Luke had explained. "They've chosen us to be their caretakers. Sometimes, these things just happen. Trust me, they don't belong to anyone in this world. They used to belong to two little elderly ladies in town. They moved into an elderly apartment complex where pets aren't allowed. That's the truth, Dad!"

The kids said the Flame Point was Muriel and the Blue-Cream was Beatrice. They acted like they met these cats before and knew them well. "Not only did they belong to sisters, Dad, they are sisters!" Nell chimed in at the time.

Oh, well, he thought, as Muriel rubbed up against his leg, waiting for a chin rub. These two are great company and wonderful relaxers for me, no matter how they arrived on our doorstep! Bea was already helping him at the computer. She was on the cabinet with her chin hanging over, waiting for her share of attention.

He was looking forward to tomorrow—the Fourth of July. They were going to the town's parade. Nell and Luke had their bikes all decked out in red, white and blue streamers. They'd be riding them with other kids in the parade. There'd be a prize for the "Best-Decorated Bike".

Lenny and Tom would come over tonight so the six of them could go by and see his and Lenny's mom, Nanny Kylahy, because she was in a nursing home and this was her anniversary. Even though she didn't remember it and she'd forget that they were there as soon as they left the Solarium because of her Alzheimer's, they liked to all go together on this day, as they did for so many years in the past.

He thought about the kids and how good they were with his mother. They were so patient and loving and wanted to see her often. She was special to them. They were only babies when this horrible disease started to take her away from them. Now that he was working from home, he enjoyed having the chance to see her more than he ever had with his old job. He'd visit her when he needed a break. Physically, she was fine. Mentally, she really didn't know what he was talking about, but he'd keep talking because he figured she liked to hear his voice. At least, she still remembered his name. Pretty soon she wouldn't.

He thanked God that Mar's mother was okay. She'd been living with Mar's brother, Joe, in upstate New York, for a good many years and had really adjusted well to the move. She got into her oil painting, sewing and knitting even more than she used to when her husband was alive. She even braided rugs. She loved using the new embroidery machine they got her. They saw her as often as they could.

As he thought about the good changes in his life, he thought about how much happier and relaxed Mar was now. He never realized how tense he made her, as well as the kids, because of his drinking.

At the same time that Mike was doing his remembering about the last few months, the children were doing theirs.

Dad and Uncle Tom had helped them to enlarge their "Secret Place," by putting pieces of two-by-fours all around in the shape of a small house. They also added steps that would safely afford them a way of climbing the tree that the hut was built against. So, they could climb the tree and sit on the solid platform Uncle Tom and Dad put there.

"I'm so happy tomorrow's the Fourth, Nell, aren't you? It's gonna be fun and exciting!"

"Yeah, Luke. I can hardly wait! Our bikes look great! I hope one of us wins a prize! Hey, if we don't—so what! I think they're beautiful!"

"Me, too! I'm even happier Dad's been getting involved in so much with us, like helping us with the decorating and rebuilding this hut with Uncle Tom."

"Oh, Luke! He's doing great, isn't he? 'Knock on wood,' he stuck to the resolution. Hasn't it been great with him sober?"

"I'll say! I know it's hard for him. But, getting away from where he worked was the best thing that could've happened to him."

"And, to us! We have him home all the time now, with Beatrice and Muriel."

"Speaking of Bea and Mur, do you think Ma and Dad really bought the story of their arrival out of nowhere, Nell?"

"The second story, not the first about their being strays. He and Ma love them dearly! Don't they?"

"And the cats love them, too."

"Oh, I know that! They're our little angels, 'bequeathed'—how's that word?—to us by Hannah. Do you remember the day we found them, Luke?"

"Yeah, and I remember that last day we saw Hannah. I'll never forget it!"

"She changed us over so quickly from being bears and rushed us to the shore of the stream, so Ma and Dad wouldn't be worried. We really didn't have much time for a decent 'Good-Bye'."

"I know, Nell. I wish we could've stayed with her longer. And, I wish we could still see her!"

"I remember her saying she'd always be with us, Luke, and I believe she is. I've sometimes felt like a gentle breeze go past my face when it isn't breezy out. I know that was her."

"Yeah, I've felt that, too. Or, sometimes I feel like someone's guiding me when I have to make a decision or I'm havin' a hard time. All of a sudden, the decision's made and it's turned out to be a good one and I don't remember really taking too much time to 'ponder' -a good word?"

"Yeah! I like pondering. I've been doing a lot of it lately. I've been wonderin' just where Hannah-Mariah lives. Remember, Luke, when we came back to get our stars?"

"Uh-huh. We had a hard time findin' them under the snow. But, wasn't it amazing how they let off a little glow, so we could tell right where they were?"

"Yeah! Then, we hid them in our rooms until the snow had melted. After a few days, we took them on our walk back into the woods."

"What a disappointment! After trudging through the snow-covered trees, without much of a path to go by, and coming up that hill, only to find that the little cottage no longer existed."

"Did it ever or was it a figment of our imaginations?"

"Come on, Nell! We didn't imagine our visit there. Hannah-Mariah was very real! She IS real! She wasn't a ghost. Didn't we find a piece of the mirror on the ground that still had the words, ' . . . forever friends' on it?"

"I know. You're right. It was real! I remember when we looked up where the chimney used to be, we saw Hannah's little bluebird looking at us from a branch of that birch tree nearby. Then, when he knew he had our attention, he flew down into that sheltered area and chirped for us to follow. And, there were the kitties, snug and warm in that kitty mini-house. What a joy it was to find them!"

"No one would believe what we saw, where we went, Luke," Nell continued, "so, it's best we tell no one for awhile. Right?"

"Yeah, I agree with you. Although, I think Ma suspects something. She saw you kick our stars into your hiding place that day. Yet, she's never asked about them. Someday, we'll tell."

"Okay, Luke, but just our family—not other kids."

"No. Maybe just Ma, Dad, Uncle Tom and Auntie Len. You know, Nell, I can't believe the changes in our lives since that day! Not only do I truly feel the presence of someone guiding me now, whether it's Hannah or my Guardian Angel she told me I have—but, with Dad being sober and no screaming and playing all those games with him over letting him have the keys or getting rid of the bottles when we'd find them—it's like a relief, like a heavy pressure's been lifted. You know what I mean?"

"I hear you. The same goes for me. I feel less drained. I have more time and energy to devote to my schoolwork. I get to get more sleep. We never got much, did we, Luke?"

"No, Nell, we were always worried. We never knew when he'd go off, what would trigger it—a holiday, a birthday, your recital—"

"You know, Luke," Nell cut in, as if her life depended on getting this thought out. "I really think those AA Meetings help Dad tremendously!"

"Oh, I do, too!" Remember the first anniversary one he let us go to with him and Ma. I'll never forget all the food—the desserts. Wow! That was great!"

"Meeting all those nice people was fun, too, wasn't it, Luke? Sometimes, you couldn't tell who the alcoholics were in the families. A lot of times, the wives or husbands of the alcoholics looked worse than the ones who drank."

"You know why, Nell? They had been through the wringer emotionally, just like the children. Do you remember that teenager who got up and spoke?"

"Yeah, she was sad, Luke! So young to get hooked on that stuff. Weren't you proud of Dad the night he got up and spoke? He was great! He had a lot of people teary-eyed, besides us."

"I know. He's quite the speaker! It's good for him to get up like he did. I hope he speaks more often. I like to hear him. When he told them he was lucky to have gotten off the liquor now—before he became too addicted, and, then he went on to say how it's because of his almost losing us that he 'stopped cold turkey', I felt good! Our disappearance was beneficial for Dad. Hannah knew what she was doin'."

"I guess! I thank God every day and I keep asking him and our angel friends to continue to keep Dad sober. It's like a miracle to me!"

"To me, too! Some people don't believe in them, but I sure do! Not many alcoholics can stop like that. I realize, too, Nell—we both have to—that there really isn't a cure—but, I'm willing to take what's happened to him 'one day at a time', the AA way."

"Oh, I agree, Luke! Hannah worked some kind of magic. Let's leave it at that! And, we should never take Dad's 'sobriety'—another good word, huh?—for granted."

"I know. Hey, we've been sitting here, yackin' away and haven't noticed the time. Now, thanks to Ma's thoughtful little Taz Clock here, we can see and we had better head back."

"Okay! Let's get goin'! Hide the clock."

* * *

On the Fourth of July, Mike, Mary, Leonore, Tom and all their neighbors and friends stood by the side of the road, watching the kids on their gaily-decorated bikes. They were at the end of the long parade.

One of the town's two new fire trucks led the parade with Uncle Sam riding on back near the ladder, waving and throwing candy to the kids who were watching. It looked like the same guy who did the Santa ride on the fire truck up and down the neighborhood streets at Christmas-time.

An Atkinson Police Car kept a nice distance behind the kids, so that they'd be safe.

Behind the fire truck, there were lots of people dressed in the red, white and blue in all types of clothing and homemade costumes, walking along. Some were dressed in Stars and Stripes. Some made themselves animal costumes, so people wouldn't recognize them and they could act as wacky as they wanted to, waving and dancing and doing whatever would get the bystanders applauding and laughing.

There were clowns, too, dressed in the three colors in a wide array of clown clothing—from the big shoes to the teeny hats with their bright red noses and happy or sad faces.

Some people walked their dogs and had them dressed for the occasion, too.

When Luke and Nell spotted their family, they waved and smiled, being careful not to lose their balance and fall or bump bikes with the children in front of them.

They all ended up at the town common, which had been newly enlarged last year. There was a platform set up that was decorated in lots of pretty red, white and blue bunting. It was something that'd be put away for any other events at the Village Green. The decorations could easily be ripped off and re-done.

As the kids stood around this platform, with their folks easily gathering in the background, a tall man with a beard got up to the podium. It was John Henry Harriman, the Town Councilor, who also worked as a volunteer fireman.

John Henry spoke about the happy occasion and all the great costumes on the people and the animals. Then, he praised the kids and their families for coming up with the fabulous ideas they had for decorating their bikes. He said it was so hard to decide on three winners because they all looked great!

"But," he went on, "I finally narrowed it down to the 3 most originally decorated and decided on: 3rd Prize goes to Kathy McKenna because her bike looks like a carriage with that hood and the sides with those open windows; 2nd Prize goes to Nell Kylahy because of the way she made her bike look so silvery and has it shiny through the flag design to look like a star has burst forth; and, 1st Prize goes to Luke Kylahy, with his most original stars—all silvery, shining and sparkling through the Betsy Ross flag design he has perched on the back of his bike. Would the three winners, please come up here?"

Nell, Luke and Kathy all ran up to the podium. John Henry handed each of the children a ribbon and a gift certificate to Toys R' Us, the toy store in the nearby town of Salem. The kids thanked him and smiled as their parents and all the other bystanders applauded.

Nell was no longer self-conscious about smiling. She now sported shiny new braces that she didn't mind wearing in the least. They meant something special to her.

Just as she and Luke were staring down at their family, they saw something that looked familiar—yet, didn't. Because there were lots of people dressed as animals, they almost wouldn't have recognized her—Hannah-Mariah—standing right between their mom and aunt, smiling away at them and winking. She was a little shorter than they were. Ma and Auntie Len never noticed her.

Hannah had her hands on something in front of her. It was hard for Luke and Nell to see just what because of the crowd of people surrounding them. They had to know what she was holding and almost broke their necks trying to peer way back there and down.

Finally, they saw what she was touching. Each of her paws was on a shoulder of the two little bears in front of her—Nell's look-alike, with turquoise eyes and a ponytail and braces on her teeth, smiling and waving up at them—and, Luke's bear-twin, with baby blue eyes and bandages on his paws.

As the children went to jump off the platform, the music began and something really magical happened. Nell's large silver star and Luke's smaller ones on their flags all started to sparkle and glitter and pop right off the paper—and, lift up into the sky and float away.

Luke and Nell made it over to their parents and aunt and uncle, just as this started to happen.

As they got closer, Hannah and their bear doubles lifted off with the stars smiling and waving. Nell and Luke smiled and waved back excitedly. They could no longer hide their excitement and awe over what was happening from the people near them, who were mesmerized.

Everyone watched the stars go flickering upward, in the early evening sky. Only Nell and Luke watched the bears who were with the stars.

People wondered why these two children were waving at the stars. Oh, well, they're only kids, the townspeople thought.

Somehow, Mike and Mary seemed to sense it wasn't just the stars that leant a mystical touch in these early evening hours. They sensed there was someone who returned here tonight to check on the kids he or she met and touched in some way six months ago.

Both parents knew there was a change in the children—nothing obvious, something subtle. Plus, there was also a change in them. They prayed that whoever that was disappearing upward would always be there for them and Luke and Nell. So, they waved and smiled, too, even though they couldn't see anyone.

Nell and Luke turned when they could no longer see Hannah and the little bears and caught their mother and father waving. Their parents went to put their arms down, but weren't quick enough for their kids. So, they smiled, gave Luke and Nell a loving knowing look and hugged them. Then, they proceeded to help them move their bikes to the truck with Leonore and Tom, as if this were an everyday happening for the Kylahy family.

The rest of the people in town just stood there gaping at the holes where the stars were in the kids' decorated bicycles. They couldn't speak.

Auntie Leonore and Uncle Tom weren't let in on Mike and Mary's thoughts. But, that was okay because they had their own questions, as they followed Mike out of the small dirt road near the town library, adjacent to the grass parking lot.

"Did you sense there was more to those stars flying up in the sky, Len? I sure did!"

"You know, Tom, something's been different about the four of them, since the kids' disappearance back in January. I know Mike's been good with his promise and that's great! I just feel a certain—I don't know how to put it—'glow'—about them. It's like they're being guarded and protected. Do you get that feeling?"

"Yes. That's it exactly—a 'glow', an energetic spirit in all that they do, even the little things!"

"I know what you mean. I think it rubbed off on us, too, because I sense help always being there for me, if I only ask."

"Me, too, Lenny. I was afraid to ask you. I thought you'd think I was crazy. Oh, well, maybe it's the Guardian Angels we were told we had as kids. Maybe, that's who saved Luke and Nell."

"Maybe, that's who they were waving to right now, Tom."

"Maybe," he said, as Len and he rode in their Bronco, gazing at the stars in the early evening sky— particularly, at the big one with a small one on each side of it. These stars seemed to hover directly above the Kylahy truck.

Lenny stared happily at the flickering stars. She could've sworn she caught the look of a face smiling at her on the biggest one. It must be my imagination, she thought. Only the man in the moon showed a face, not a star. Then, she thought she saw a wink. She looked over at Tom just in time to catch him winking back.

They looked at one another and laughed.